MW00941507

The Chosen One

Christopher Allen Walker

Copyright © 2019 Christopher Allen Walker

All rights reserved.

ISBN: 978-1-0860-4720-2

The Chosen One
By Christopher Walker

Convict Chris Brandin, by chance, writes to an overseas address that will change his life forever and make him The Chosen One. He meets a Korean beauty who's looking for a pen pal but finds love… Chan Que is a South Korean businessman getting up in age who needs to find a son-in-law to expand and take over his empire… Brandin considers himself the luckiest man on earth after Chan gets him released, offers him his only daughter and his business, only to find himself in the middle of a war and in the sights of one of the world's most feared hit men….

ACKNOWLEDGMENTS

First off I want to thank the All Mighty for keeping myself and faith strong, I want to send thanks to all my fellow convicts that read my material and pushed me to get it published, form Pasquotank, Central, Nash and Folsom prisons, keep your head up, my editor Ms. Norman, family and loved ones, Moms, Sherri, Brandin, Brandi, Donea and my reason for striving Alivia Christiana, thanks for your support and unconditional love.

Chapter 1

"Yo, Chris," Justice hollered through his cell door.

"What's up?" Chris asked.

"If you send me two stamps to mail this letter out, I will send you five overseas addresses to some Korean, Philippine and Japanese women. They will write back and send pictures too."

"That's a bet. I will send the stamps up by c/o Barnes, send the addresses back down," Chris said.

Chris Brandin was on ICON which means Intensive Control for getting in trouble in population here at Pasquotank Correctional. He had to be there for six months. Twenty-three hours lock down, so he figured he might as well write and receive as much mail as possible.

"Barnes? Yo, Barnes! Take these two stamps up to Justice's room. He's sending me some addresses back down."

C/O Barnes came back about 10 minutes later and said, "Lay the fuck down," and slid the addresses under Chris' door. Chris picked the addresses up off the floor and hollered back up at Justice.

"Yo, Jus, how long does it take for them to write back?"

"About a month." Justice answered. "Make sure you fill out the envelope right and put USA under or beside your address."

"OK," Chris hollered, "but I'm looking at these addresses and I ain't fixin' to burn my stamps on these bitches if they ain't going to write back!"

He decided to write just one of the names on the list and wait for a response, then go from there. He looked at the list and picked out Lin Que with a South Korean address. He went ahead and filled out the envelope and put the stamp on it. He liked to write late at night, so he put it up until later. It was 6:00 pm and time for the 6 o'clock gutter mix with D.J. Stress out of Virginia, 92.1, and he definitely had to have that.

Chapter 2

South Korean Border – One Month Later

"Lin, Lin, wake up Lin! You're going to be late for class!" Lin finally rolled over and glared into her maid's face.

"What time is it, Myra?" Lin asked.

"It's 7:30, you have 30 minutes to get yourself together and get to school."

"Oh shit!" Lin said and jumped out of bed and rushed to the bathroom.

Downstairs her father, Chan Que, was sipping his tea and staring into his bowl of oatmeal. His mind was in another place, another time. He looked out across his second-story deck to the hills, trees, and mountains of North Korea. He had purchased this mansion just for the outstanding view and because he liked to sit and observe both sides of Korea and reminisce about when he first met his wife...

She had been a Columbian news reporter when he was still a Staff Sergeant, in the South Korean Army. He knew he had to somehow win her heart or die trying. But as destiny would have it, Lynn Richardson had already noticed the handsome Korean watching her. So, she surprised him by approaching and saying, "Hi, my name is Ms. Richardson of the Diplomatic News Team out of Columbia. I'm doing an article on the North and South Korean armies. Would you care to have lunch with me?" The rest, as they say, was history. They married six months later and got a nice apartment inside the South Korean city limits. Chan attended his official duties while Lynn wrote freelance articles for different magazines in Columbia. Lynn didn't associate with her family back in Columbia because she did not approve of their business dealings. That was the main reason for her staying in Korea. She and Chan had a beautiful daughter and named her Lin after her mother but spelled in the Korean tradition. All was happiness until North and South Korea declared war against one another thus leading to outside military forces taking matters into their own hands. Terrorist acts were reported every day from both sides and that's how Chan lost his soul mate, his beloved Lynn. She was enroute to the Korean news building when she was caught in crossfire. Her Range Rover was hit by missiles launched from the enemies. That was the end of Chan Que's happiness and the start of his criminal career. His only regret in life was that he didn't have an heir, a son, to carry on his namesake and take control of his empire. He loved Lin with all his heart, but he couldn't let her know the truth of his business dealings. His loyalty was forever with his late wife. Even though other Korean men would have found another wife to bare their heir, a son, Chan could never see himself being with another woman. His soul mate was in another life and that's where his heart would always remain. His only hope would be in his son-in-law, whomever his daughter chose to be her husband. This would be the one to follow in Chan's footsteps and take over his business affairs. So that is what was on Chan's mind this morning. Would his son-in-law be man enough to handle his affairs? Would he have the heart to succeed? And most important, would he be able to expand the business to the US like Chan wanted?

"Papa?" Chan turned and looked at his only child. He always felt a squeeze on his heart when he looked at

Lin. She had his Korean nose and slated eyes, long, jet black hair but that was it. The rest was from her Columbian mother. The big, pretty, gray eyes and full lips. The dark tan complexion that was year-round. All this gave her the exotic look that stood out among her pale Korean friends. Chan had chosen to raise her in a western way as well as Korean to show respect to her mother. Lin was only 3 years old when her mother was killed but she remembered her loving kisses and hugs and felt the emptiness in her chest when she looked at her pictures around the house.

"Papa, why are you looking at me like that?" Lin asked.

"I'm just amazed at how you've grown up on me. Your mother would be so proud of you," Chan said. "Now before you are late for school, give your father a hug and kiss and let me know what you want for your graduation."

"You know I don't care about that Papa," Lin answered. "Anything you get will be fine."

Chan walked over to the phone on the night table, pressed a button and told Myra to send the car around to take his daughter to school. Lin kissed her father, told him she loved him and was off to school. Chan had enrolled her in private school that taught English as well as Korean. In a few weeks she would be graduating and off to college, which Chan wasn't looking forward to because he would definitely miss his daughter. Especially if she decided to go to college in the United States, which Chan already guessed she would. After all, she did have her mother's blood in her veins.

Later in the evening, Myra interrupted his thoughts with the days mail. He had a few important notices to tend to, but one caught his attention because the stamp on

7

the back in red said it was from the Department of Corrections in North Carolina. He turned it over and looked at it. It was addressed to his daughter, Lin. What the hell? From an inmate in a prison in the US. Someone by the name of Christopher Brandin. Now how in the hell did he know Lin and how did she know him? Chan decided that he would ask Lin just that when she came home. Until then he would check this guy out and see what he came up with. He also had a governor friend from North Carolina that he could contact if needed. Chan strolled down the stairs to his study room. The computer was always up and running. Korean words flashed across the screen as he searched for information on prisons in North Carolina. He easily found a web address that any citizen could use to find out an inmate's parole dates or hearings, past criminal history and present charge(s). The web address was www.ncdoc.com. Chan used the information from the envelope to enter the man's name and inmate number. Once he entered the information, he was rewarded with a picture and history of Christopher Brandin that read: Light skin black male, 5'7", 165 lbs., green eyes, currently serving 17 to 23 years for attempted murder plus an 8 to 11-year term for armed robbery! Currently on ICON status for dealing drugs and soliciting an officer at Pasquotank Correctional. Release from ICON in 4 months, projected release date from prison June 2022. Chan stared at the man's picture on the screen and asked the question to himself, 'How do you know my daughter?' He would definitely have to find that out as soon as Lin came through the door.

Chapter 3

"Lin, your father wants to see you in his study," Myra said.

"Ok, just let me put my books in my room," Lin answered. Chan was on the phone when Lin knocked on the door.

"Hold on. Who is it?" Chan asked.

"It's me Papa. Myra said you wanted to see me."

"Oh, come on in, sweetheart." Chan abruptly ended his call to focus on his daughter entering his study.

"What's up Papa?" Lin asked.

"How do you know a Christopher Brandin?" Chan asked.
"I don't," Lin answered.

Chan knew that his daughter doesn't lie to him, so he passes the letter to her and asked, "So how can you explain this?"

She looked at the letter confused at first, then breaks into a smile. "Oh, Papa, I forgot I put an ad for pen pals on the internet just to meet some new people from the United States."

Chan realizing that he had overreacted, said "Why did you do that?"

"I just wanted to meet some new pen pals from the US," Lin answered.

Chan got up and went to the computer. He showed Lin what he found on the internet. "Is this the type of person you want to be pen pals with?"

Lin looked over his shoulder and said, "Well, it's only writing letters and he is locked up. Besides, he is pretty cute!" When she saw her father's expression she said, "But if you really don't want me to write back to him, I won't Papa, I promise."

This made Chan feel guilty. He realized that Lin would be 18 years old soon and could make her own judgements. "No, it's ok, Lin. I was just concerned and trying to look out for you. I guess I'm just getting used to you being grown up. Here's your letter. Do as you please."

 "Thank you, Papa," Lin said as she kissed him on his cheek and left the study. Chan had a few more calls to make before his meeting this evening with one of his oldest clients. He also wanted to have a few drinks and maybe even get a palm reading: something he hadn't done in years.

Lin went to her room and changed into some silk shorts and top with a matching robe. She laid across her bed to read the letter from her new pen pal. His name is Christopher which she already knew from talking to her father. He says he's in prison for robbery of a Mexican drug dealer. He writes poetry and likes sports, especially basketball and softball. He also works out five times a week. He tells her to stop reading and pull his record and picture up on the internet, which she does. Now she has the same picture and information her father had. He says he hopes to hear back from her soon and to include a picture of herself. Then, at the end of the letter, he writes a poem. It's titled: "Precious Moments", about when you see a woman for only a second out of each day but just her smile and pretty face will ease your pains and chase your troubles away. Lin doesn't realize that once she starts reading his poem, everything else around her is tuned out. Her phone is on its eighth ring when she finally finishes the poem and jerks to answer it.

"Hello," Lin answered. "Oh, hi girl. What's up with you?" Lin asked her best friend from school, Nikiro (Niki for short).

"What am I doing? Well, I'm sitting here reading a letter from a convict in North Carolina."

"How does he look?" Niki asked.

"Check for yourself," Lin answered, as she gave Niki the web address.

"Oh, he's sexy for an African American," Niki said. "What did he say?"

"Nothing much; just explained his crime, but he did send me probably the sweetest poem I've ever read in my life," Lin told her friend.

"Well, read it to me! You know I love poetry."

Lin reads the poem to her friend. Saying the words again, she feels them deep in her soul. When she finishes, she asks Niki, "What do you think? Niki? Are you still there?"

"Yeah, I'm here," Niki answered.

"Well?" Lin asked.

"I think you should go find him in the US and marry him, prison or not!"

They both laughed at this and after gossiping a few more minutes, hung up with goodbyes. Lin had no homework today, so she decides to write Christopher back. She tells him she is 18 years old, getting ready to graduate and would soon be off to college. She wants to come to the US for college but doesn't want to leave her father in Korea alone. She also loves sports and believe it or not, she has 50 Cent and Slim Shady's latest CD's. She tells him about her mother and that she is half Columbian and half Korean and how his poem really touched her. She says she hopes that they can be good pen pals and write a lot. She sends him one of her school pictures and a graduation picture taken at rehearsals. Lin was feeling tired now, so she addressed the envelope and put it on her nightstand. Just before she turned off her computer, she looks at his face; really his eyes and she smiles. As she lays down for her afternoon nap, the last thing that crosses her mind are the sweet words of his poem "Precious Moments".

Chapter 4

"Myra, please have the car brought around. I have a personal appointment this evening."

"Yes sir, Mr. Chan," Myra said going to the phone in the kitchen. Chan put on his black silk coat with matching pants and slipped his feet into his black wing tips. Then he sighs and takes off his coat on the way to his walk-in closet. He pulls out a metal box and takes a shoulder holster and slips it on. Then, checking the clip on his Beretta 9MM he slips it into his holster just for precautions. He thinks 'you never know what might transpire' he learned that after seeing his wife killed for being in the wrong place at the wrong time.

"Mr. Chan?" says Myra through the door. "Your car is ready and waiting."

"Thank you, Myra. Please tell Lin I'll be back late so no need for her to wait up. Also, see if you can find out what the girl wants for her graduation. I'm having a hard time selecting something."

"I will try Mr. Chan, but we both know she already has everything and doesn't care for most of that. She is just a free spirit. But I will try," Myra stated on her way back to the kitchen.

Chan walked through his house down to the garage where his Benz limo was waiting. His regular driver was a young kid whose father was from his old army platoon. The kid's father didn't want his son in danger, so Chan pulled some strings and got him a job as his driver. The young man stood by the back door holding it for Chan.

"Good evening, Mr. Chan," the young man stated as

Chan settled into the back seat. He told the driver to take him to General Yao Hai's palace in the hills of North Korea. Chan knew he would be in enemy territory by being from South Korea, but his reputation and his dealings with the General made him untouchable among the North Korean armies. Only a fool with a death wish would try to harm the second in command of the Untouchable Korean Mafia. General Yao and Chan Que supplied all of China, Japan and North and South Korea, along with a few other countries, with pure white heroin, called China White in the streets After Chan's wife's death, his best friend from childhood, Yao Hai, became the General of the North Korean army and took over the underground heroin operations. Yao took his best friend's grief over the loss of his wife personal. He told Chan that if he joined forces with him, using Chan's overseas connections to expand the business, he would do everything in his power to find out who and what group had bombed and killed his wife. Chan, seeking revenge, hastily agreed. The North Korean underground terrorist group, the NK*Lords or North Korean Lords, were a small unit of about 50 men that were responsible. Word quickly spread when the group and all its members suddenly disappeared from the face of the earth. Every underground group and network knew who was behind their vanishing act. That was why no questions were asked.

Chan's limo pulled up to the palace gates and was buzzed through. It is a beautiful palace built into a mountain opening with enough security one would think the floors were made of gold. Yao was a cautious man but, in his trade, he would live longer being cautious.

Chan told his driver to blow the horn twice and proceed through the gates as they opened. Chan knew they were being monitored every step of the way. The young man drove through the gates with ease and stopped by a concrete waterfall in the middle of the palace grounds. Chan exited the limo and made his way to the palace entrance. As soon as his feet touched the steps, the doors were opened by a beautiful young maid. She bowed to Mr. Chan and stepped aside to let him enter. Yao was seated with his legs crossed at the end of a white marble table.

"Please join me," Yao said as he poured tea in Chan's cup. "Let's get straight to business," Yao spoke in perfect English. He hardly ever used English unless talking about the business because all his servants spoke Korean and didn't understand a bit of English. "Chan," Yao started, "we have a healthy supply of heroin in need of a buyer. We both have discussed extending our operation to the Eastern coast of the United States, but we have yet to find a person to oversee this enterprise and find us the valuable customers we need," Yao stated very seriously. "We are both getting up in age where we must make the proper moves to secure our family's futures and their family's futures after them and so forth. I can't father children and would never adopt to carry on my bloodline. But you, you have a chance. Even though I know your heart rests in the afterlife with your wife, Lynn, you still have a chance through your daughter. You must choose wisely and make sure the man who takes her hand will accept and know his responsibilities. Does Lin know that it's tradition for the father to pick her husband?"

"I've given her freedom, but she understands that

when the time comes, he has to have my approval," Chan stated. "But we have both agreed that I'm not going to force her into anything. My love for her is too strong to force her into anything. She turns eighteen in two months and then to me, she is a woman. So, until then, we wait and see how things develop. I know patience is the key but believe me, the choice will be made."

"Ok," Yao said. "I will leave your family affairs in your hands. Just update me on any man trying to win your daughter's hand so I can check them out. Remember, she is my God daughter too." Chan, sensing these were Yao's departing words, rose and bowed to his best friend. He then quoted their Korean Mafia words; "May Our Families Love Remain Untouchable." Yao bowed his head and Chan exited the room.

Back in his limo, Chan instructed his driver to take a right which led them to a small village called Shangtown with shops on the edge of the small paved road. Chan knew that the lady he wanted to see had a shop at the end of this street. He had been here, once right before he met Lynn. The old lady had held his palms in hers and told him to keep his eyes open, because he would soon meet his soul mate. Now as his driver opened his door and walked into the small shop's entrance, he wondered what the woman would tell him today. The shop was a small room with a desk and old worn out chairs. In the back was another small room closed off by beads hanging in the doorway. A small Korean man asked him if he was to see madam Wyson and Chan said yes. The old man gave him a glass of whiskey to ease his pulse and motioned for him to proceed through the beaded entrance. As his eyes adjusted to the dark room, he noticed the old woman sitting at a small table.

"I knew you would be back soon," she said.

"Soon!" Chan stated. "It's been almost 20 years."

"Yes, so soon. Don't you agree?" the old woman answered, smiling. "Sit down and give me your hands and let me study them a minute." Chan sat down and laid his now sweaty palms in the old woman's hands. They were always cold. It felt like holding hands with a corpse. She closed her eyes and hummed to herself for the next five minutes. Then she opened her eyes and asked Chan, "what troubles you sir? What family problems hinder your sleep at night?" Chan wasn't surprised by the woman's knowledge. He knew she was an old legend and not a fake just out for the money.

"I have problems with my family business," Chan stated. "I have to pass the knowledge of my family trade, but I have no male heir, only a daughter. So, whomever she decides to marry must carry my family name and expand my trade to the US" She laughed, which caught Chan off guard. "It's really an important matter," Chan said getting a little upset.

The old lady applied pressure to his hands and said" I know your family business is important. I meant no disrespect with my laugh, but you're concerning yourself over nothing. The one who will carry your family trade and expand it to the US. He already knows the trade and your daughter's already in love with him because of his words, 'Precious moments'. Please be safe and come again real soon." Chan, realizing he was being dismissed, left the usual 500 on the table and without a backward glance, left the room.

On the way home, his mind was racing over every detail of the day's events. How did he see his son-in-law today when he never went anywhere but to meet Yao and to his wife's grave and now to this small village? He looked at the back of the head of the young man driving the limo. No, he doesn't even live with Chan. Only Myra stays with them but maybe on the drives to school..." Excuse me, young man," Chan said. "Your name is Mouli, right?"

"Yes sir," Mouli said.

"Have you ever spoken to my daughter about anything on her rides to and from school?"

"No sir. We never say any more than 'Hi' and 'thank you," the young man said. My father made it very clear to do my job to the best of my ability and respect your family at all times."

"Do you ever see her talking to any guys around the school?" Chan asked.

"No sir, they won't let any guys hang around the all-girls school because of some assaults last year on a female student."

"Alright, it's not like I was asking you to spy on her because I trust my Lin, I was just curious," Chan added and sat back to gather his thoughts. The old lady said something about Precious Moments. Was she trying to say that his Lin was no longer a virgin?! He had already had the birds and the bees talk with Lin. She said she knew from her sex education class in school so he guessed he would just have to ask her. He knew she wouldn't lie but if she was having sex, then, whoever he was, he better be ready for marriage or death.

Life was full of choices, Chan thought as the limo pulled into his garage and the young man jumped out to open his door. Chan thanked him with a generous tip and proceeded into his mansion.

Chapter 5

It was about 10:00 pm and the house was somewhat quiet. He figured Myra was in her room, so he went into the kitchen and fixed himself something to eat. There was a dish left over for him, so he heated it up in the microwave and filled his stomach. He went to check on Lin. As he approached the door, he heard her talking to someone. Probably Myra or either she's on the phone, he thought. He knocked on the door and asked if he could enter.

Lin said, "Come in," and he came into her room. She was in her bed, looking like the little girl he remembered, talking on the phone. He pointed at his watch and she nodded and told her friend she would see her tomorrow and hung up. Chan got right to the point of what was on his mind.

"Lin, have you been seeing any boys?" Lin looked at her father surprised.

"No Papa, why do you ask that?"

"I was just wondering because I know guys notice you and since you will legally be a woman in about two months...I know how hormones are at your age..." Lin's eyes got big.

"Papa! Are you asking me if I've had sex?!"

"No, well, I, well, I just want you to wait until you're married, that's all Lin," Chan said.

"Papa, I haven't even French kissed a boy much less had sex. Guys aren't too turned on by my looks compared to an olive-skinned Korean woman. I lose out because of my darker skin and exotic look. Besides, my grades and college are more important than dates right now. Why do you think I put that ad on the internet pen pal page? It's nice to hear from people around the world. You can decide who to write to or not. Either way, you are in control of the friends you pick."

Chan asked, "By the way, did you write that Christopher Brandin, the one in prison?"

"Yes, I did," Lin answered. "But I haven't heard anything back. The poem he wrote me was very touching. I wish I could find a guy to tell me that our time together is all precious moments." Chan's head snapped around.

"What did you say?" Lin, looking confused about her father's reaction, said it was the name of the poem Chris had written her.

Chan said, "Ohh," and got up from her bed. "Alright, you get some rest, so you won't have to rush off in the morning," he said, leaving her room.

He still didn't understand the old lady's meaning on how he had already met his son-in-law that day. As he entered his study, he sat down at his desk looking at his computer screen flashing about NC prisons. On impulse he pulled up the file of Christopher Brandin. The face flashed back on the screen and Chan printed everything about the man's record. Chan started to really read the printout in his hands, and he started to see where the future was headed. Christopher Brandin had robbed the so-called Mexican Mafia and gotten involved in a full-blown shoot out. His co-defendant was serving a 30-year sentence, while he had 25 years. All sentences were under appeal. The Mexicans had turned state's evidence on Chris and his crime partner, which was against the code of the streets. Chris held his own and had even started selling drugs on the inside, something that was never proven, but an officer's statement and confidential informant's word got him put on Intensive Control lockup for six months. Chan looked at the young man's face. He had never been biased as far as a person's skin color was concerned but he remembered how some of the Korean people had looked down on him for marrying his wife, Lynn. He didn't want his daughter to have to go through that same pain, but he already knew that fate's hands were dealing the cards and that the old woman was never wrong in her wisdom.

Chan picked up the phone and dialed his friend, Yao. Once his maid put him on, Yao asked what he needed. "I need a first-class flight booked all the way to Vicks Airport in Virginia Beach, VA. Call me in the morning with the times," Chan said.

"Does this have to do with our business?" asked Yao.

"Everything," Chan answered.

"Then I will make sure everything is handled right away," Yao said.

"One more thing" Chan said. "Call our Senator friend in Washington and arrange a special visit with an inmate named Christopher Brandin at Pasquotank Correctional Institute in Elizabeth City, NC for later this week."

"Done," Yao said.

"And May Our Families Love Stay Untouched," Chan said as he hung up.

Chapter 6

Pasquotank Correctional Institute, Elizabeth City, NC

"Brandin! Chris Brandin."

"Yo!" Chris hollered back at the officer standing in front of his cell door.

"Get dressed. You got a special visit in 10 minutes."

Now, who the fuck is that! Chris wondered. They must have slipped cause my visits are suspended for 6 months along with all my other privileges. He got up and washed his face and brushed his teeth (not like they can smell his breath because all inmates on ICON status lockup visit behind a glass – non-contact). But he felt better without the dragon breath. Two officers came and put a waist chain around him and connected it to a black box around the handcuffs. Now he was transported like Hannibal Lecter, to the non-contact visiting booth which consisted of a small room with a stool to sit on in front of a plexiglass window and a phone to talk to the people on the other side. They removed the chains and handcuffs and locked him in the room. Chris' visitors weren't on the other side yet, so he sat down on the hard ass stool to wait. He figured it had to be Mom Duke or his sisters or maybe this older chick Brenda he had known for a while or maybe this young broad named Jenny from Cali. They were the only ones who wrote him occasionally or came to visit. He heard the door on the visitor's side open and he looked up as an Oriental man entered the booth and sat down. Their eyes met and locked as he reached for the phone. Chris did the same. Chris said, "You must have the wrong booth or something unless you are one of my

22

lawyers' new partners."

Chan just looked at Chris, sizing him up for another minute. Chris was beginning to think that the man didn't understand English. Then the man spoke in perfect English. "My name is Chan Que and I know everything about you and why you're in here."

"Well, that's just great Mr. Hue, or Que or Bruce Lee or whoever you are, but I don't know shit about you or what the fuck you doing here to see me," Chris snapped.

Chan just smiled and said, "But you do know of my daughter."

"Your daughter? No! I don't know your daughter or...Hold the fuck up," Chris realized. "You are Lin Que's father from Korea?" Chan nodded. "Damn, you came all this way to tell me not to write your daughter?"

"No," Chan stated. "I came all the way here to tell you to marry my daughter and help expand my family business."

Shocked into silence, Chris couldn't say one word. Chan told him his entire story, how he lost his wife and was too loyal to re-marry. How whoever married his only daughter would be his heir. When Chris finally got his voice back, he asked the first question that popped into his head.

"Why the fuck did you choose me? I mean out of all the people in your country and the United States, why me?" Chan had figured this would be one of Chris' questions, and he was ready to reply.

"Because the work of my family business requires loyalty and trust, also a man who has heart. I studied your case and saw where you didn't take a plea to testify on your co-defendant and instead, went to trial even though you knew your chances were slim. That shows a lot about your character."

"What the fuck do you mean, character?" Chris snapped. "That's my way of life. Death before dishonor! I will never do the cops job for them! I was raised with the thought that if you get caught, you do the time, but you don't run your mouth on the next man!"

"That's exactly the reason you are the chosen one," Chan stated.

"By the way," Chris asked, "What kind of family business do you run?" Chan shook his head and said he couldn't discuss that until Chris was out.

Chris laughed at this and said, "First of all, I got 8 to 11 years to do followed by 25 to 34 years to do with a minimum of 25 years. Secondly, your daughter is probably a very beautiful girl that I hardly think would want to be married to a convict who lives a million miles away from her."

"My daughter will do as I suggest," Chan said. "I already have a brilliant lawyer going over your entire case and I have a few friends high up."

"How high up?" Chris asked.

Chan moved closer to the window and whispered," Put it this way, my company donated a large sum to Dale Simms Governor's campaign."

"What! He's the fucking Governor of the state!"

"Be quiet!" Chan whispered. "I know who he is, and I also know that I can get you out of here in the next six months. But I want to know that you will protect my daughter with your life and die trying to make her happy and I want to know that you will always be loyal to me and help expand my business to the U.S."

Chris moved in real close to look into Chan's eyes before he spoke. "Mr. Chan, if you get me out of this hell hole, I will marry your daughter and run your business no matter what it is! And that's my word and my word is Bond." He and Chan locked eyes for what seemed like eternity, neither one looking or turning away.

Chan spoke and broke the silence. "I feel I've made the right choice but there is one thing that must not happen."

"Oh shit!" Chris said, "I knew there had to be some bullshit caught in this. It was too sweet to be true!"

"No, nothing like that", Chan answered. "I only want you to promise me you will protect my daughter and never let her know the business we conduct."

"Hold up!" Chris said. "You want me to marry your daughter, protect her, build a family by taking over your business but she can't know what the business is? That's crazy! How the fuck do I hide your family business from her and what the hell is the business anyway?"

"I told you it can't be discussed in here. All I can say is that there will be a front, a cover for you to use around her and others," Chan stated.

"Oh, ok. I guess I can handle that," Chris said.

"No," Chan stated. "Look me in the eyes and promise me."

So, Chris looked the man in his eyes. The man who was offering him his daughter and his business. The man who was getting him out of the belly of the beast before he turned 50 years old. He promised to hold his end down or die trying. Chan stood, bowed and said, "You are the chosen one. May our family's blood remain untouched."

Chapter 7

"Hold up Lil' Nigga, now run this crazy story by me one more time," New York said. Chris and New York were walking around the yard. He had been let off ICON, released back to regular population and was enjoying exercising his legs after being locked down for six months. Chris and New York had started their bid together. They clicked because they both liked the same things, money and bitches. New York was family, so after Chris got off lock down, he found New York and told him about the entire visit with Chan Que.

"This Chan Que said he has the fucking Governor in his pocket and can get me out in six months, but I have to take over his business and marry his daughter," Chris said.

"And he wouldn't tell you what the business was?" New York asked.

"Nope," Chris said. "He said he couldn't discuss It in here."

"Damn, nigga, he might be in the drug game or in some smuggling guns type shit," New York said. "That might be why it's such a secret."

"What the fuck does it matter?" Chris said. "Either way I won't be wasting away in this hell hole. I wouldn't give a fuck if he wanted me to merk the President long as he gave me my freedom."

"Just make sure you don't forget fam," New York said. "What! Forget fam, nigga, if this is what I think it is and Chan Que got pull like he say he does, then my nigga, you coming out wit me, that's how I get down!"

"Word!" New York said.

"Word!" Chris said as they gave each other dap.

Chris got back to his cell, smoked a blunt to clear his mind on what he was going to say to Chan's daughter when she wrote back. She might be 4 feet and 300 pounds, but it didn't matter, cause he had already given his word. He should be getting a return letter from her real soon and maybe even a picture.

At 2:00 pm, mail came the next day. Chris got a return letter from a Miss Lin Que in South Korea. He started to rip it open and realized his palms were sweaty and he was nervous as hell. 'What the fuck is wrong with you?' he asked himself. You been a player all your life, now you getting shook over some Korean chick! Shit! He opened the envelope and unfolded the letter. A picture fell out on his bed face down. He started to turn it over then thought it better to read what she had to say first. She had pretty handwriting he thought as he read how she liked volleyball and softball and would be graduating soon. She said she hoped I like the picture and that she really liked my poem, Precious Moments, and looked forward to reading more of my poems. She said she didn't have a boyfriend because she went to an all-girls school and studying and homework took up most of her spare time, but she would answer all my letters and write as much as possible. She said her and a friend were excited about seeing the US. They were coming to the United States in about a month to tour some colleges in Washington, Los Angeles and New York. She ended the letter by saying that she would keep me in her prayers, and everyone makes mistakes and not to give up on life because she would always be there to write. What I got out of reading her letter is she was a good person with a good heart so at least my words will be taken to heart, Chris thought.

Well he might as well see what his future wife looks like. He picked up the picture and turned it over. Everything in his body froze! He stopped breathing and all sounds ceased to exist.

This couldn't be…. He was looking at the most beautiful girl he had ever laid his eyes on in his 25 years on this earth. Chris had let his mind build up a stereotype of a pale Korean with slanted eyes and an overbite and that was too far from the truth. Lin Que had the dark complexion of a person from Hawaii or Costa Rica; definitely not pale by a long shot. Long black hair falling down past her shoulders that even in a picture looked like silk. Her eyes were a light shade of gray. But even all that couldn't compare to the full lips that she had. To sum it all up, not a dime but a twenty-cent piece. A fucking Goddess! How in the hell was he going to make this girl fall for him when she could have any man on this planet? Even though it was going to be hard, he still had a big advantage, her Dad in his corner.

Right now, he had to write back and send her another poem that would catch her heart and tell her how beautiful she really was. The he had to write Mr. Chan and tell him to give Lin permission to visit him when she comes to the US. Then if she decided to see him the rest would be up to his charm and his words.

Chapter 8
South Korea

"Mr. Chan, you have some mail that just came in," Myra said as she handed him the letter.

"Thank you, Myra. Have you contacted the people about my daughter's graduation present?" Chan asked.

"Yes," Myra said, "everything is in order for her graduation. Anything else I can get you?"

"No thank you, that will be all." Chan waited for Myra to close his door and opened the letter from Christopher Brandin. As he read the letter, he smiled to himself at what the young man was requesting. He had to admit that the man had heart and he would see that he got his wish. He had to be calm about things so that Lin wouldn't know that he had already visited Chris. Chan picked up the phone and called Myra in the kitchen. He told her to send Lin up to his study as soon as she came in from school. Chan sat back in his chair and thought about the visit he had with Chris. He saw what he wanted to see in the young man's eyes. Loyalty. Chan knew that Chris would do everything in his power to succeed because he felt like he owed Chan his life for getting him out of prison. As for Lin and Chris, he didn't know about his daughter's taste in men, but he had heard her talking about the poem. Chris wrote her and that was the first guy she had ever carried on about so there was a chance. Chris was a nice-looking man with green eyes like emeralds, so meeting him in person could be what Lin needed to feel the attraction. His thoughts were interrupted by a small knock on his door. "Come in," Chan said.

"Hi Papa," Lin said. "Myra said you wanted to see me."

"Yes, please sit down. We have a lot to discuss," Chan said. "How are your last days in school?"

"Oh, we are having fun planning and getting ready for graduation and I'm really excited about our trip to the US," Lin said.

"I'm glad you brought that up," Chan stated, "because I have a letter from someone requesting permission for you to visit them when you come to the US and I wanted to ask your opinion."

Lin looking at her father with confusion, said, "Who's requesting to see me and why did they write and ask you?"

"Well, it seems that this person thought it was tradition and custom to ask one's father to visit with their daughter, so he wanted to ask me first in case I had a problem with it," Chan said.

"You said 'he'. Who is 'he' Papa?"

"He is your new pen pal from North Carolina," he said. "You informed him of your upcoming trip to the US and he wanted to meet you in person, that is if you wanted to meet him. But as I said, he wanted my permission first. Which I must say I'm impressed because I see that he has respect for your family," Chan stated.

"So, do you want to visit this man at the prison and see him in person? If you do, it can be arranged when you're finished visiting the colleges. If not, then it doesn't matter to me. You will be eighteen years old in two months so it's time for you to start making your own decisions," Chan said.

"You mean you wouldn't mind me seeing him?" Lin asked.

"As I said, this is your friend and you are going to be on your own visiting colleges, so if you want to see him, then it's alright with me," Chan said.

"Well, let me think about it and I'll get back to you, but thanks, Papa for being so understanding and giving me my freedom. I love you so much and you will be missed while I'm away, but I promise to send you post cards from everywhere I go," Lin said, "And I will call you too."

"Ok, honey, just let me know what you decide. I can set up the visit through a friend of mine in Carolina. Oh, and I almost forgot, you have a letter too, from your friend," Chan said handing Lin the letter.

"Thanks, Papa. I'm going to my room. I will see you at dinner," Lin said as she kissed her father and left.

As she went up the stairs to her room her mind was going a mile a minute. Why would Chris want to see her in person? And why would he go to my father? And why was my father being so nice and helpful about me seeing Chris? All these thoughts flashed through her head but then she just considered herself happy to have a loving, understanding father. Lin collapsed on her bed to read Chris' letter. Why was she getting butterflies in her stomach as she opened the letter? She had never gotten them over a guy, any guy. He said he had gotten her letter and was glad to hear back from her. He said he wanted to ask her to visit him, but he felt that it might be too much to ask because she would be busy visiting colleges. He said he wrote her father because that was the respectful way and even if she couldn't see him, they would still be friends and continue to write. He said he was out of the hole and enjoying his exercise and freedom. She felt herself blush when he told her about how beautiful she was and how she could have any man she wanted and that he was blessed just to have her as a pen pal. He ended the letter by saying that on the next page was a poem he had written for a special someone in his life. So, since she was the only person besides his family that wrote to him, he was sending it to her. He asked her to read the poem and feel his words and know that her letters have brightened his days.

Lin went to the last page and read the title of the poem he sent to her...

-Soul Mate-

Whenever I tell her 'I love you', she feels it deep in her heart. When our eyes first meet, we will be in love from the start. When she's down or depressed or in pain Even though I'm far away, I feel the same. She will know my thoughts like an open book to read. And I know that my side, she will never leave. When she laughs, I laugh. When she cries, I cry. No matter what the future holds, my love for her will never die. I never thought that I would find that woman who would become part of my soul. But then I realize, just as I found her, she found me, and that we both are just part of God's Destiny.

Lin sat on her bed staring at the letter. A tear fell down her cheek. She had never in her life felt such love and emotion put into words before. She had always been a hopeless romantic and one who loved poetry. Just imagining Chris saying these loving words to her made her body tremble, but of course he wasn't in love with her; only writing her some old poems he had written. But still now she knows in her heart she had to see this man in person. It was like a magnetic pull. Right then she decided to go visit Chris in prison. If nothing else she would do that for him but first she had to call her best friend and recite his poem and see if it had the effect on Niki as it did on her.

Over dinner, Chan couldn't help but smile when his daughter told him she would visit Chris. Somehow, he knew that she would say yes. He had never heard Lin speak about a man before and from the look on her face she was all excited about meeting this man.

Myra came in carrying a small box with a bow tied around it and set it on the table in front of Lin. "Go ahead and open it," Chan said, "it's something small for your trip." Lin opened the box. Inside was a Platinum American Express card with her name on it. She looked at her father as he smiled at her. "That's part of your graduation present to use on your trip. It can be used anywhere and has a limit of $250,000, credited to your expense account," Chan stated. Lin jumped out of her chair and ran to her father.

"Oh! Thank you, Papa! You are the best father in the whole world," she screamed while hugging and kissing her father's cheeks.

"After you get back from your trip and we decide on your future, I will have something else for you. Remember, nothing is too good for my princess," Chan told his daughter.

Chapter 9

"New York!" Chris hollered at his man, "What the deal son? I got some shit to tell you. I got two pieces of good luck today. Let's take a lap and build."

"Word! That Chan dude move faster than a mutherfucker! Damn son, I can't believe how lucky you got on this shit," New York said.

"Yeah, and to top it off, Lin wrote me back saying she would be to see me at the end of next month when she comes to the United States," Chris said.

"Damn, I know you excited about seeing that queen, I know you can't wait to see her in person bad as she is!" New York said, licking the blunt closed. He had seen the picture she sent to Chris and still couldn't believe Chris' luck.

"My nigga, I got to put everything I know as a playa down on this visit. I mean, she already told me that my poems touched her and made her cry, but damn, I got to make this girl want to be my wife and that's deep," Chris said. "I ain't gonna front. When I looked at her picture, my heart stopped, and I had a funny feeling like she was meant to be my girl. But a nigga been on lock up for 6 years and this is the baddest woman I've ever seen. What if I get out there on VI and freeze up?" Chris said.

"Hold up Lil' Nigga, I been knowing you for five years since we started this bid," New York stated. "And one thing I know is when it comes to females, you ain't never going to freeze. So, you might as well hit this blunt and quit trippin. Put it in your head that this shorty is already yours and pull this shit off so you can get out of this hell hole," New York said.

"Yeah, you right, I'm just going to be honest as I can and let her know she got me open off just two letters. If she loved my poems, she going to love me cause the words are just a reflection of the person. You feel me?" Chris asked.

"I feel you Lil' Nigga, just like I feel this blunt and I got confidence in ya that you going to handle your business. Just don't forget fam," New York said.

"Forget! Nigga, if I have it my way, you coming up out this beast too. If Chan can use one favor from the Governor, he can use another. Once I'm out, I plan to do everything in my power to get you back in the streets. We started this shit together and we gonna end it together. Word up!"

Chapter 10
South Korea

"As you young women of the class of 2003 walk through life, always hold your head high and strive for the best," The principle ended his ceremony speech as the graduates erupted in cheers tossing their caps into the sky. Lin and Niki hugged one another and cried in joy that school was finally over, and they could start their lives.

"Damn girl, I can't wait to see some of the US. I'm so tired of this country and it's politics," Lin said. "The only thing I will miss is you and my father. I wish your family would let you come to college in the US too. Once I get settled, you can come stay with me?" Lin asked.

"I don't know," Niki answered. "You know my family. I might be able to visit some, but stay? They would have a fit! I had to beg for a month just to be able to travel with you while you visit colleges and they're still worried that our plane might crash or be hijacked by terrorists!" Niki said as they both laughed. "Are you going to the graduation party?" Niki asked.

"Nope. I'm just going to stay at home with my father and go over some of the college pamphlets," Lin said. "What about you?" she asked.

"I'll be with my family. You know how they are about parties plus they've invited family over for a get together to give me my graduation present. So, it will be just me and my family, but I will call you and let you know what I get after everything settles down, ok?" Niki sated.

"Ok," Lin answered. "Just get plenty of rest cause I'm

pretty sure we won't get any in the US. I'll talk to you later."

Lin walked to where the limo was waiting to take her home. Her father left right after the ceremony, giving her time with her friends. As she settled into the back seat, her mind wasn't on college or the places she would see in the US, but on what she was going to wear to visit Chris. Again, she felt the butterflies rolling in her stomach and smiled at the building excitement.

Once she got home, she was greeted by Myra and her father holding a big birthday cake with eighteen candles on it. "No wonder you left in a hurry," she said to her father.

"We decided to celebrate your birthday and graduation since you will be away," Chan said. "So, you have to make a wish and blow out the candles." Lin closed her eyes and blew out all the candles, then sat down to eat cake with her father.

"Lin, we have to talk. I wanted to wait until you came back but by then you will already be eighteen," Chan said. "You understand our custom and our family ways and you know that I've tried to raise you by our Korean ways and respect your Mother's memory and allow you your freedom. That's why I decided to let you go to college in the US and have a life of you own. Our Korean ways would have you marry a Korean husband and be a housewife and for my grandson to take over my business in the foreign car trade. I won't force you to be a housewife and take away your freedom, but I want you to know I'm getting of age and my business needs to expand to the US. I just want you to know you have my blessing if you found a husband in the US to settle down with."

"Father, I don't want to disappoint you or the family custom, but I don't have finding a husband on my mind. I'm concerned with my future and what college best suits me," Lin said. "I've never even kissed a guy so how would I go about finding a husband? I mean, I love you so much for the freedom you've given me, but I just don't know about the husband thing."

"No sweetheart, don't get me wrong. I'm not saying ask every man you date to be your husband. I'm just saying that if you meet someone and fall in love, then you've got my blessing," Chan said.

"I will keep that in mind" Lin said, "but the only guy that's been in my thoughts lately is doing 30 years for armed robbery," she said laughing.

"Suppose he wasn't in prison and you could go out on a regular date with him. Would you go?" Chan asked. Lin stopped laughing and looked at her father.

"That's funny you should ask that when just a few months ago you were asking what I was doing writing a convict in prison. Now you want to know if he were out, would I go on a date with him?"

"No, I just wanted to know if you like or start to like a guy, would you pursue it, that's all," Chan answered.

"Well, I guess the answer to that is 'yes'. I would go on a date with Chris if he were out since our two-hour visit is going to be like a blind date anyway. I am looking forward to meeting him." Lin said.

"I just wanted you to know how I feel and that I'm always here no matter what you decide. I plan to be doing a lot of traveling to the US when you start college, so we won't be apart too long," Chans said. "And as long as you're happy, then I'm happy. So, don't be worrying about your father. Now I must make a few calls, so I will see you later." Lin started to get up, but Chan stopped her. "Lin, I love you with all my soul. While you're gone please take care and just follow your heart. It won't lead you wrong."

"Ok, Papa, I love you too," Lin said as she kissed her father and left, wondering what brought on that last statement.

She went up to her room to finish going over her plans for her visit to the US. She and Niki were flying First Class from Korea to LAX airport in Los Angeles and spend two weeks visiting colleges in LA and Sacramento. Then they were to fly to Dulles in Washington, DC to spend another week exploring Georgetown Law School. Lin had decided to make Washington, DC the last stop because it was only a 3- or 4-hour drive to Elizabeth City where Chris was being held. Her father had informed her that a visit was scheduled for the Friday of the last weekend in the month. So, everything was set. But two things were bothering her. One, was that she knew her father had given her a chance to have a life and not be a bored housewife. She understood the Korean customs. These ways were why her best friend Niki couldn't go off to college. She was already promised to the son of a wealthy Korean family. She would be rich and never want for anything but her freedom to do as she pleased would end when she said, 'I do'. Lin couldn't think of being married off having to stay in South Korea her entire life and for that she was grateful to her father. She wished she could meet a guy and marry someone who wouldn't mind his wife pursuing her own career and going to Law school. But what man wouldn't object to all the long hours and the long trials? The thought came into her head like a lightning bolt. 'What about Chris!' What if she asked Chris to marry her? Then she could go to college and continue her career and visit him on the weekends. Then her father wouldn't have to worry about customs because she would be married at eighteen just like all the other Korean girls. But would Chris say 'yes'? He might feel like he was being used. But she really liked Chris even though they hadn't met. The butterflies in her stomach were a sign if nothing else and his poems were so heart felt she wanted to tell him face to face she loved his words! But would he agree? What would he have to gain? She could use his case as research and try to get him back in court. But what if she did get him back in court and he got out? Would he stay with her or leave? Damn, her mind had so many unanswered questions but somehow, she knew she had to at least ask him for help. She would tell him the entire story, the whole truth, and then ask him to marry her. God would her father be happy if Chris said 'yes' and she could get married. She knew that meant a lot to him so if nothing else worked, she would try money. Money always got things done in America. With her plan set in motion, Lin laid down for an evening nap. Right before she drifted off, she said a silent prayer… God, please let Chris accept me as his wife to be. Please. Amen.

Chapter 11
Los Angeles, California

"My feet are killing me," Niki cried, "these shoes are so pretty but they are hell on your feet, especially when you've walked all over California in them."

"Yeah, but you weren't thinking about that when you were strutting your stuff for those college guys," Lin teased.

"It was all those tanned bodies that took over my mind," Niki stated. "I couldn't go to college here in L.A. cause I would never get any studying done," she said as they both laughed. Lin and Niki had been to both Sacramento and Hollywood to different colleges and had decided to relax at the Beverly Hills hotel in L.A. and do some shopping before leaving for Washington, DC the next day. "Well, what do you think of the big Sunshine State?" Niki asked.

"They have some impressive colleges here, but I'm like you. It seems to be a lot of partying and hell raising than studying and I'm trying to become a top rate lawyer, so I don't like the atmosphere," Lin answered. She didn't tell her best friend that she had her mind and heart set on Georgetown in DC so if her plans worked out at least she would be closer to Chris. Besides, Georgetown Law School was one of the best law schools in the country. "Well, maybe Washington will be better that this," Lin said.

"I just hope the guys are this adorable too!" Niki said. "I should have brought my camera. The girls back home would've loved to see some of them."

Chapter 12
Dulles Airport, Washington, DC

As Niki and Lin got off the 747 in Washington, a limo was waiting to take them to the Trump Plaza where their room was booked. They enjoyed the sights of the Washington Monument and the ride past the Pentagon and the White House. They decided to turn in for the day due to the long flight and start fresh in Georgetown tomorrow. Lin had a hard time concentrating because her mind was on the upcoming visit with Chris. They had arrived on Tuesday, so she had only three days to get her thoughts together as to how she was going to pop the question. From her visit to Georgetown, she already knew one thing, this was the law school for her. Regardless of what the outcome would be between Chris and her, she was enrolling at Georgetown Law School.

"I knew you would like this place. I can tell by your eyes," Niki said. "But what else is on your mind, Lin? I know you like a book."

"I guess it's my first visit with Chris," Lin explained. "I'm just so nervous because I really want him to like me. You know I've never really had any kind of feeling for guys but every time I think about Chris my stomach flutters!"

"What!" Niki exclaimed. "Are you trying to tell me you have developed feelings for this guy? A person you haven't even met!"

"Yes, I like him but...but it's something else," Lin stuttered.

"Something else! What do you mean, something else?"

Niki asked. "Are you saying you are in love with a convict who writes nice letters and poetry? Lin! Look at me!" Lin looked at her lifelong best friend and she couldn't answer yes or no because she didn't know the true answer herself.

"I don't know what I feel, Niki. All I know is it makes me nervous as the days go by. All I want is for him to like me."

"Lin, believe me, he will like you. I've known you all my life and I've never heard anyone utter a bad word about you. Besides, he's been locked up a while and you're a beautiful girl so believe me, he will love you," Niki said.

"I hope you're right," Lin said.

Chapter 13
Elizabeth City, NC

All Friday morning Chris had been a nervous wreck. He had gotten a fresh haircut, went and worked out but nothing could calm his nerves. He wanted to blaze a blunt bad, but he didn't want to go out to visit with his eyes all red. His eyes were one of his best features and today he would need all his abilities to pour on his charm.

"Yo! Lateef! Didn't you say you had some new cologne from the streets?" Chris asked.

"Yeah, Cee, what's up? If you getting a VI or something, you can use some," LA said. "It's that new shit out by rapper, Cam'ron, Ooh! Boy! Word."

"I preciate that my nigga, I owe you one." Chris said.

"Knowledge, knowledge," LA said, handing Chris the bottle.

Later on, as Chris was in his room drying off, he heard his name over the PA system to report to visitation. Well, here we go, he said to himself as he dressed in his new pressed prison browns and slipped his feet in his black Timberlands. He popped some Winterfresh gum in his mouth, got his ID card and put a dab of Ooh! Boy! on and headed for the visitation room. Lin was a nervous wreck herself. She wished she had let Niki come in with her, but she and Chris had personal things to discuss so she wanted it to be just them. She had heard them page him to visitation a few minutes ago but she was trying to calm herself and slow her heartbeat. She took another sip of her drink and waited to meet her future husband face to face.

Chris had to go through a side door and check in where an officer wrote his name down and searched him. Then he was let into the visiting area. Once inside he had to check again with an officer in the front area of the room to have his time logged in and he was told where his party was sitting. All this is done because like today it was packed and sometimes it's hard to find the people who came to see you. The officer logged him in at 1:05 pm. That meant he had until 3:05 pm – two hours.

"Brandin, your party is at table 3 from the drink machine," the lady officer said. He turned and started walking on legs that seemed to have turned to stone, towards the tables.

She was at the table with her back to him so he walked up behind her and touched her shoulder and said to her beautiful face, "Hi Lin, I'm so glad you could make it!" Lin was sitting with her back to the officer's desk. She had heard the side doors open but didn't look back to see if it was Chris. Her heart was still beating too fast. She thought about going to the restroom to freshen up but then a slight touch on her shoulder made her look up into a face that was saying he was glad she could make it. For a second Lin just looked up into his face, at a sexy smile and pretty green eyes that she really wasn't prepared for. She was frozen. Her mind was saying, 'get up and give him a hug, move, do something'. But for what seemed like eternity all she could do was nothing. Then things snapped back to her. She exhaled a breath, stood up and smiled at him. He gave her a strong hug and kissed her on the forehead, sending sparks all the way to her toes. (All this she would remember in detail later.) He asked her how her trip was.

"Fine," Lin answered as they both sat down. Chris still had her hand. He never let it go when they were seated. "I've seen so many colleges these past few weeks that I might just join the army," she said as they both laughed.

"I want to thank you for taking the time out to come see me," Chris said. "I would give anything to be able to take you on a nice date with a good dinner and a movie but under the circumstances..."

"It's alright," she said. "I wanted to meet you too, so it doesn't matter the place, but I do wish our first meeting was some place nicer."

"By the way, what's wrong with the guys from Korea? Are they blind or gay?" Chris said as they laughed again. "I mean, Lin, you're a beautiful girl. If I had you as my woman, I wouldn't let you out of my sight, more or less, the country!"

"I haven't had any time for dating or anything else," Lin said looking into Chris' eyes. "I plan to become a lawyer and I've had to maintain an A+ average to be accepted into law school."

"By the way, did you choose a college to attend yet?" Chris asked.

"Yes, I've chosen Georgetown Law School in DC. That's like 3 1/1 hours from here," Lin said, looking into his face to see a reaction. There was a twinkle in his eyes that made her mind up. She decided to go ahead and be straight forward and honest with him. "Chris, there is something I have to tell you, something we have to discuss," Lin said.

"Hold on," Chris said. He didn't like the sound of what she wanted to talk about, so he wanted to say what was on his mind first. "I have something to say to you too. If you don't mind, may I go first?" Chris asked. "Sure," Lin said. "I just hope it's not any bad news."

"And I hope you don't take it to be bad news either," he said. "let me start by saying this; my days have been a lot brighter since we started writing. I've never been happier than when reading your words. When I first got your picture and looked at it, I had trouble breathing. This is no lie. I've been incarcerated for 6 years. I've had a few close women friends, but I haven't gotten serious about any of them because they either find someone else or get tired of waiting. Then you came and you are more than any man could want as a friend, girlfriend or wife."

At the word 'wife', Lin's stomach did another flip as she held her breath. "I don't know how to say this so that you will take me seriously, but you've been on my mind day and night after just two letters. I will admit I had doubts, that is until I came to this table and looked into your eyes. Now I know the truth. I'm in love with you, Lin. I love you with all my heart and soul and I want you to be my wife until death do us part," Chris said. Lin just stared at Chris as tears ran down her face. She couldn't find her voice. Chris was confused by the tears, so he just went ahead with what else he had to say. "Please don't cry, Baby! I didn't mean to upset you. I was only laying my heart out to you..."

Lin shook her head and said, "No, you didn't upset me. It's just that..."

"I know," Chris broke in. "I know I'm locked up but that's the good news I've been waiting to tell you, Baby. My case is being reviewed in 60 days and my lawyer said it looks good that I might be out in a few months." Now Lin thought she was going to pass out for real. She had to take a swallow of her drink to regain her composure. Everything Chris had said was swimming around in her mind. He was getting out! He wanted to marry her! She closed her eyes, took a few deep breaths to steady herself, then she looked into his eyes.

"Chris, I want to ask you some things and please be honest, ok," Lin said. "If you did get out and I were to become your wife, would you be here for me through the long hours at the office and long trials?" she asked.

Chris leaned over and took her hands into his and looked deep into her eyes. "Lin, Baby, if you were my wife, I would stand by whatever you chose to do. Any night, no matter how late, I would be there waiting," Chris answered.

"And you wouldn't want me to be at home as a housewife?" she asked.

"No, you can have kids whenever you feel you are ready. Even then we can always have a sitter to handle the kids. The choice is yours," he said.

"Ok. What about my father? What if he wants you to help run his foreign car trade?" Lin asked.

"Baby, I will need work once I'm out anyway and if your father can help, I would appreciate it. So that's not a problem either," Chris answered. "I might have to take some college classes to help me but all that can be done. Now let me ask you one important question, Lin, and I want you to answer truthfully. Do you love me or have any feelings towards me?" Somehow Lin knew this would be asked and she had thought about it long and hard.

"I have two yeses to your question," Lin answered.

"What do you mean, two yeses?" Chris asked.

"Yes, I will marry you and be your wife and yes, I do love you!" Lin answered.

"What?" Chris asked, not sure he believed his ears.

"I said yes, Chris, I'm yours," Lin said standing up, opening her arms for him to hug her. When she was finally in his arms, she knew her choice was right. She looked up into his eyes and said, "I love you."

When Chris heard those three words his heart filled with joy and he bent and kissed her soft lips. Pure heaven is what he felt. When their tongues touched, she let out a little moan, so he had to break the kiss and remember where he was. Lin just stood in his arms; eyes closed for a few seconds as he stared at this beautiful angel God had sent him. When she opened her eyes and saw Chris staring at her, she could see and feel the love in his eyes. She wanted so bad to take him with her back home and never let him go. She knew she had to speak with her father about his special contact friends in America to see if any help could be given about his case when it came up for review. She realized that in the last two hours her law degree had taken second seat to getting her future husband out of prison. Wait until she told Niki. She was going to flip her lid!

Around them, visitors were beginning to say their goodbyes as they both looked to see the clock read 3:00. "Time goes fast when you having fun," Chris said. "I plan to write your father tonight to ask for your hand in marriage. That should give you time enough to break it to him. I hope he will accept me."

"Don't worry about that," Lin said. "He gave me his blessing on that subject before I left home. I'm going to see if his powerful friends over here can help you with your case too, but I will write you every day until you're out, I promise." she said.

"Just take care of yourself and have a safe trip home. That's all that matters to me," Chris said. "Before you go, I just want you to know I will always love you and do my best to make you happy and take care of you till I leave this earth."

"I know, I know you will. Don't make me cry any more, please Chris. It's already going to be hard waiting. You have to understand that you are my first love and I want you out of this place!" Lin said.

"Visitation is now over. All visitors please exit the visiting area," the officer announced over the intercom. Chris and Lin kissed again as they headed for the doors.

"Oh," Lin said, "can you use the phones?"

"Yeah, why?" Chris asked.

"Cause I want you to call me Thursday at 4:00 or 4:30 pm."

"May I use your pen please?" Lin asked a female officer. She wrote her number on his arm.

"I'll try but if I don't, it's because they sometimes trip over the phones in here, but I will write, ok?" Chris said, "Ok, I love you," Lin said, leaving the room.

"I love you too," Chris told her.

Chapter 14

3 Months Later

"Damn! York, I can't believe this day is here," Chris said as he gave New York five and a hug. He had gotten a letter from the Supreme Court throwing out his attempted murder charge and giving him time served on his robbery charge. He was to be released that morning at 9:00 am. Lin and Chan were picking him up. "Lil' Nigga just take things out there slow, day by day. You got a winner for a wife, a fucking beauty queen. Just do right by her and build on your future. And don't forget your fam in here."

"Never that!" Chris said. "You my first concern when I find out what Chan's business is about. Either way, I'm going to ask him to go to his Governor source for one more favor. So just to be on the safe side start putting the word out that you won an appeal and your case is back in court. So, if and when you do get out, no one will make any fuss on the inside because we still got to slip the haters. They hate to see a real nigga get a break. You just maintain and don't let these lames get you in trouble. Right now, my nerves are on edge so let's blaze this last blunt together and then we gonna talk some shit to these bitches on the way to receiving." Blowing nothing but weed smoke, Chris said, "I got a lot to do and a lot to plan. I chose not to tell my Mom about all this cause I didn't think Chan was serious and didn't want to get her hopes up. So now, first and most necessary, I got to go see Mom Duke and introduce her to Lin and tell her we are to be married and everything. She's going to be happy for me but Momma ain't stupid. She will pick up on the dirt if I do something, so my game got to be tight all the way around."

New York passed the blunt back to Chris and said, "All you got to do is take advantage of what Mr. Chan is going to offer. His daughter said he was in the car trade or something, so whatever it is, it's clean money, so you ain't got to worry about being in the streets again and if it is some dirt involved, you can handle it cause you real. So, either way, you can't lose. Let's get ready to bounce my Nigga. It's 8:45 am. You 'bout to be a free man in 15 minutes. Just do me one favor."

"What's that?" Chris asked.

"When you finally get up in that ass, hit it one time for me my Nigga. Word up!" York answered.

"No doubt my Nigga! No doubt," Chris said as he gave New York another pound.

Chris put all his letters and addresses in one bag. He had given everything else away. Others had been at him all night for whatever he had to give away, so his cell was empty. He gave a bag of mail to New York as they walked to receiving.

At the receiving door, New York and Chris exchanged pounds and hugs. He told New York to look for a letter within a few weeks with his new address and phone number. Then he disappeared through the receiving door. At receiving, he had to sign a lot of papers. Then they went through his property. He had told Lin to send clothes in his sizes and he was curious to see what taste she had in style. The officer brought out a box with his name on it and gave it to Chris. He opened it and was impressed at what he saw. Inside were a pair of red leather Timberlands, size 9 ½ as he asked. Also, a Sean

John black sweater and Sean John blue jeans with a red leather belt to match his Tims. He also had a black and red leather Avirex jacket with the fox hoody attached. He was like a kid at Christmas getting out of his prison browns and putting his new clothes on. Everything fit perfect. After he was dressed and signed more papers, the officer asked if he was ready to go. Chris laughed and said he had been ready 6 years ago. The officer had to escort him out the front to the party who had come to pick him up. He grew more nervous with each step. He had to take deep breaths to calm himself. When he got to the front office, he again had to sign saying he received his forty-five-dollar gate check. After that, the guard told him he was free to go through the front doors. Chris took another deep breath and pushed through the doors and was stopped dead in his tracks by what he saw. Parked right in front of the Gatehouse was a black, stretch Benz limo. As soon as his eyes got from one end of the limo to the other, the doors opened, Lin jumped out and ran into his arms. Once she was in his arms kissing his face, the Benz and everything else began to fade. He could see her black, silky hair that smelled of peaches. He could feel her warm body against his, a feeling that even on past visits over the years, he hadn't felt. When he opened his eyes, her father was standing behind them with a smile on his face. Chris broke the hug and stepped to Chan.

"Mr. Chan, it's so nice to finally meet you. I can't thank you enough for all you've done"

"You've done your share," Chan said, "you've made my daughter happy and my family happy so I would say we're about even. I like your clothes. I see my daughter has good taste."

"Stop, Papa. You know you helped me pick out the clothes over the internet."

"So, good taste runs in the family," Chris said.

"Well, I know you're ready to get away from this place," Chan said, "so let's ride. You said you wanted to see your mother first so I take it we will be traveling towards the Greensboro area? Please input the address into the car's OnStar system." Chan told the driver as he held the door. They all climbed into the back of the Benz which could have seated 10 more people with ease. Chan sat across from Lin and Chris. "There's a wet bar if you would like something to drink," Chan asked.

"No thank you," Chris said. "I don't really drink. I stopped that before I got locked up because we used to race Mustangs on the weekends and bet major money and it's kinda hard to change gears, hit the nitro and hold the horse in the road even while sober."

"So, what are your plans now that you're free?" Chan asked.

"Well, I want to go back to college and finish up this Business Management class I started in prison. I figure whatever your business, I can use the knowledge to help you expand."

"What about Virginia?" Chan asked. "I knew you were born there but Lin has picked out a nice house in the Georgetown area. Would there be a problem with you living there?"

"I think it's perfect, but Georgetown is really in the D.C. area, but that's still good with me cause Lin will be close to school and I'm not that far from my family." Chris answered.

Lin had been quiet so far just listening to the

conversation. Her mind wasn't really into what they were saying but on her wedding date and when it would be set and what would happen once, she and Chris were alone.

"What about the house, Lin? Did you like it?" Chris asked.

"What? Oh, yes, it was beautiful," she answered. "It's in the uptown area of Georgetown. Five bedrooms, three baths and a big basement that you could turn into anything. Also, it has a beautiful swimming pool outside and a nice fenced off backyard."

"But, of course, it's only temporary, right?" Chan asked, "Because I know once you're familiar with my business and start making your own profits, you will want to build yourself a home to be more secure in your surroundings. Right Chris?"

"Of course," Chris answered, "but we will have to decide on the location, but as long as Lin's happy, I'm happy."

Chan explained to Chris about the foreign car trade and how he wanted to bring five new Toyota car dealerships to the East coast; one in New York, Miami, Richmond, Texas and Maryland. He said the company in Korea had designed a new, state of the art Toyota 2005 Spyda with everything from four wheel traction control to a drop top at the push of a button and as soon as he could get the dealerships open and running, he could start shipping the cars. He explained that the hardest part of the work would be done by the dealership CEO's, but Chris' job would be to oversee the shipment of the new Toyotas. He said they would discuss it more in detail. Lin finally got into the conversation about her being accepted into Georgetown Law and how she wanted to be the first Korean Attorney General. Chris didn't miss the tightness on Chan's face when she spoke of this. He filed it away for later when they would speak alone.

It was about 1:00 when they finally exited off Hwy 40 into Greensboro. Chris' Mom lived right outside of Greensboro in a small town called Reidsville. She had a nice two-bedroom house and worked hard to take care of it. Chris, his Mom and two sisters had been together since his father passed. His Mom had worked hard to provide for them. He still felt that he had let her down by going to prison, but she was always there for him no matter the situation, right or wrong. His youngest sister, Nicole, was living in the next county with her boyfriend and his oldest sister, Denise was married and living in Reidsville also. As the limo pulled into the driveway, he saw an all too familiar Honda and knew his Mom was home. She had always owned a Honda since he was small because it was good on gas. He knew she was probably asleep because she worked 3rd shift at a nearby textile plant. Good. He could wake her up and surprise her.

 "Listen," Chris said as he took Lin's hands, "don't be afraid of meeting my Mom cause she's down to earth. You will see."

"Oh Baby, I understand but I'm still nervous. What if she doesn't like me?" Lin asked.

"Don't worry about that. She always told me that as long as I'm happy, then she's happy and you make me happier than anyone else," he said, "so relax."

Chris got out of the limo. A few of his Mom's neighbors were in their yards staring but he reminded himself that this was the country and they probably hadn't seen a Benz limo except on TV. So, he smiled and gave them a wave and proceeded on. A big yellow dog of some kind stood under the carport and gave a warning growl. Chris stopped and searched his mind to remember a name. "Hey Rocky, come here boy," Chris called as the dog came to him with his tail wagging. He rubbed the dog's head and went up to the front door and rang the bell. He waited two minutes, then opened the storm door and knocked on the inside wooden door. He got butterflies in his stomach as he heard footsteps walking through the house. It had been almost a year since he had seen his mother on their last visit, so she was excited. She had always told him not to give up faith in God because she knew he wouldn't have to do the entire 30 years. Something good was bound to happen. And here he was out, free, and at her door. A face appeared in the small glass on the door. She looked half asleep into her son's eyes, then her eyes got big and she ripped the door open and jumped into his arms.

"Oh Baby! I can't believe it's you," Chris' Mom hollered. He stepped into her living room smiling as his Mom kissed his cheeks with tears of joy running down her face.

"I wanted to surprise you Momma but please don't cry."

"What! How? When did you get out?" she asked.

"Hold on," he said, "okay, sit down cause I got a lot to tell you. Then I want you to meet some people."

Chris explained from start to finish how he wrote to and met Lin, how Chan helped him get out and how Lin and he had fallen in love and they were to be married.

His Mom looked him in the eyes and asked, "Do you

love this girl, Chris? I mean really love her enough to settle down?"

He looked back into his Mom's eyes and answered, "Yes, Momma, its' not like any feeling I've felt before. You always said as long as I was happy, you would be too. I am Momma, I am," Chris answered.

His Mom stood up and walked to the door and said, "Well then, it's settled. Now let me meet my soon to be daughter-in-law and thank the man who got my son out of prison."

"Ok, but Momma, Chan doesn't want Lin to know that he helped me out because he wanted her to love me on her own even before she knew I was to be released."

"Oh, ok," she said as they hugged and went out the door to meet Lin and Chan.

Chris went to the limo and opened the door for Chan. When he looked into Lin's eyes, he could see she was tense. He grabbed her hand and smiled to let her know everything was fine. Chan got out and walked up to meet Chris' Mother. His Mom opened her door to let in the Korean man. Chan walked into her living room.

"Please have a seat," Chris' Mom said. He took a seat on a black leather sofa. "I don't know what you did or how, but I just want to thank you for helping my son," she said.

"Your son is my son and I know he will be able to help my family business expand. My daughter happens to be in love with Chris also, so we are both happy."

"Where is your daughter anyway?" she asked. "What's taking them so long?"

"Lin was really nervous about meeting you," Chan said. "She thinks you won't like her."

"The way my son spoke of her, I already like her, so she need not worry," she said opening her front door. "Chris! Bring that girl in her so I can meet my future daughter-in-law," she hollered.

"Come on Baby girl. I know you're nervous, but you will see that everything's fine," Chris said to Lin as he took her hand and pulled her out of the limo. Lin took a breath and followed him up to the front door. The dog, Rocky, was at her heels, tail wagging happily.

She smiled and said, "At least the dog likes me." As she and Chis burst out laughing. Chris went into the living room where his Mom was standing, waiting.

As soon as she saw Lin she smiled and said, "Hi, I'm Chris' mother Patricia and I want to speak to you in private. Follow me please." Lin looked at Chris and he just shrugged so she followed his Mom into the kitchen area getting more nervous along the way.

"Have a seat please," she said. She and Lin sat across from one another at the kitchen table. "I've spoken with my son and asked him how he felt. Now I want to do the same with you. My son has been through a lot of hard times and I love him to death. How do you feel about him in this short time you two have known one another?" she asked.

Lin looked into the woman's eyes to calm her nerves before she spoke. "Chris is my soul mate and I love him with all my heart. From the first time I read his words, I felt something that has grown even in the short time we've known one another. I would still marry him in prison but now that he is out, I definitely want to be his wife."

"What will you do if I don't approve of you?" Chris'

Mom asked.

"Nothing," Lin answered. "With all due respect, we will just have to split our time with Chris cause I love him and won't be without him." His Mom smiled and took Lin's hand and stood up from the table.

"I see that you are serious about my son," she said. "Please take care of him and you will always have my blessing."

"Thank you," Lin said and gave her a hug. "I hope you will help me with the wedding plans because I'm really at a loss and will be in need of some female insight," Lin inquired.

"Honey, after his sisters find out he is free and getting married, you will have plenty of help especially from his youngest sister, Nicole. She loves the ground he walks on."

"I'm looking forward to meeting his sisters," Lin said as they walked back to the living room where Chris and Chan were sitting.

"Miss Brandin, I want to ask a favor of you if you don't mind" Chan said. "Your son and I have a lot of business to discuss and I would like Lin to stay here for tonight. That way she can meet his sisters and get to know them. If it's a problem we can get a hotel room, but I will feel a lot better with her around family."

"That's not a problem, Mr. Chan. She can stay here as long as she wants," Chris' Mom answered.

"She has her credit cards and we will send the limo back as soon as we get a car so you can go shopping together tomorrow if you like," Chan said.

"Don't worry, we will find something to do with our time. Just please have Chris come back soon because once his sisters find out he is out they are going to want to see him."

"I understand," Chan answered. "We will be back by noon tomorrow." Chris got up and hugged his Mom again.

"I love you and I will see you tomorrow. Take care of my wifey."

"I will Baby," his Mom answered.

"Chan, I will be right out. Just let me speak to Lin for a second," Chris said.

"I will be in the limo and again it's nice meeting you, Miss Brandin," Chan said. "Nice meeting you too and please call me Patricia since, like you said, we are going to be family."

Chris took Lin's arm and lead her into the kitchen. "You will be alright here. Just chill and we will be back tomorrow."

"I'm ok," Lin answered. "I'm looking forward to meeting your sisters and taking them shopping."

"Just make sure you leave the mall before you are broke cause they will buy everything in sight," Chris laughed as he took her in his arms and kissed her lips. "I miss you; I love you, never forget that," he said.

"I love you too, Chris." Lin answered. "See you tomorrow. Call me later." Chris left the house and jumped into the limo with Chan.

Chapter 15

"Ok, Mr. Chan, where we off to first?" Chris asked.

"Our first stop is the DMV to get your license renewed, then we're going to get you something to drive so we can send the limo back to your Mom's," Chan said. "We aren't getting a rental. I'm going to get you something straight off the lot brand new, so you need to decide what you want by the time we leave the DMV. Call it an early wedding present."

"Mr. Chan, you've done too much for me already. I can't accept a new car. How would I repay you?" Chris asked.

"You will repay me through our business so relax and decide what you want," Chan answered.

"Oh, I know what I want. My dream car but can you afford it?"

"What is it?" Chan asked.

"A 2005 Porsche 911 Turbo. Starts at about $80,000. $80 or $90 fully loaded," Chris said jokingly.

"I'm sure that car will be on the lot at a Porsche dealership. If not, we can always order it and use another one until it gets in," Chan said. "You're going to need insurance, so I added you to mine so we won't have any delays at the DMV."

"Damn, you serious!" Chris said as he stared at Chan.

"When you see what the business is all about, you will know just how serious," Chan said staring back at Chris. They went to the DMV where Chris had to retake a driver's test and show proof of insurance. Then he was issued a new driver's license.

From there they hit Hwy 40 to Paul Jones exotic car dealerships and Chan paid cash out of his bank account for a 2005, Blue Metallic 911 Porsche Turbo. They were loaned a black 911until the blue one was ordered. The dealer made sure it would be delivered in seven days or less thanks to Chan's hefty tip. Chan sent the limo and driver back to Chris' Mom's house and he and Chris jumped into the Porsche and went to look for a place to discuss business.

"So, where should we go?" Chris said, shifting from second to third as the 911 sped down Wendover in Greensboro. It was the smoothest ride Chris had ever driven. He made the right choice. He couldn't wait till the blue one was back so he could sit it on chrome.

"Are there any massage parlors around here?" Chan asked.

"Yeah, but they mostly cathouses where you pay for everything and get the works," Chris said.

"That's the kind of place I want," Chan answered. Chris just smiled and got off on East Bessemer and pulled in front of a building with Chinese writing on it.

"Here's one of them. I never did know what the writing means, but the place is off the hook and safe," Chris said.

"The writing on the building says, 'A Thousand Pleasures' so let's see if it's true," Chan said smiling. They went into the building and told the Chinese lady at the front desk they wanted a room in private to discuss business. Then they wanted the works.

"Hundred dolla a piece," the lady answered in broken English.

After Chan paid, they were led to a room with a jacuzzi

in the middle. They were given silk robes and told to ring the bell on the table once they were ready for the works. Chan and Chris both stripped down and got in the jacuzzi and settled back to enjoy the hot jet pressure water.

After the water had relaxed them, Chan spoke first. "Chris, I want you to listen and listen good at what I'm about to say because once I leave to go back to Korea this operation will be yours to run and you will be dealing with a lot of money. Some clean but mostly dirty but once it gets back to me, it will be as clean as a newborn baby. My company in Korea makes Toyota cars and ships them to our main dealerships in the US. Right now, we just developed the new Toyota Supra Spyder and will be shipping the cars to all our dealers on the East coast. But," he said as he looked straight into Chris' eyes, "that is all a front my son. I push China White heroin. Mostly I've dealt with China and small things on the West coast and Midwest because I never trusted someone to make the move for me on the East coast. I was always saving that for my son because it doesn't involve risk as the other parts of the US. This is where you come in. You will be acting President of my main company in Richmond, VA so all the product will come into your dealership and it will be the five major cities along the East coast that have Toyota dealerships. We will handle the delivery and everything. All they have to do is make sure the money is straight. I can send five hundred keys of uncut heroin a month. Each key will wholesale for $100,000 apiece. Each key can be stepped on up to five times so the buyer will have no problem making 15 or 20 million off each key. You will have to handle 50 a month. Ten of it off the top is yours. I will show you how to wash and invest it wisely so don't worry. What I need to know is can you find me the players to push 100 keys a piece a month? It will be up to you whether to front some or not. That will be your business to handle. So, do you think you can handle this?" Chan asked.

"I can handle it, but I will need your help on some things," Chris answered. "For instance I need you to call another favor in from your Governor friend and see if you can get my man Lawrence Hilton from New York, out of prison that would be my first connect and we maybe could re-route some of the product through the New York dealership. That is if you've got a Toyota dealership in New York," Chris asked.

"That's a good idea. I will get on that today and yes, we have a dealership in Manhattan NY," Chan answered.

"I have fam that I've done time with in Maryland, Miami, Charlotte and Texas. And with New York in with that bunch, we could definitely put the East coast on lock," Chris said.

"We have dealerships in every place you spoke of except Texas and we can open one if needed so that's not a problem. You need to contact your players and get them on planes or busses to come and talk. Don't attempt to discuss anything over the phones," Chan said. "they will be talking straight to you. They will never see me so from this day forth, everything goes through you. Now let me explain how you and your friends will get the heroin from Korea," Chan said. "You are familiar with the 18 wheelers that transport the new cars to the dealerships? That's how we will transport the product, but the secret is the tires. There will be five new Toyotas on each trailer with five keys in each tire, so each truck will carry 100 keys. The key will be sealed inside the inner tube of the tire with Xnanox, a rubber sealant that the dogs in customs can't even begin to smell past. Once the trucks get to the dealerships, the cars will be taken inside, and our man will change the tires and unload the product. That way even if something goes down, the police will never know how we get the drugs past customs. Each of the cars will come by freightliner through Norfolk shipyard and be unloaded on the docks and shipped to your dealership in Richmond. Then we transport from there. Nothing leaves until all the heroin is paid for. Even if you decide to front, make sure you have half the money. Understand?" Chris nodded. "Now, enough business talk. Let's have some pleasure and see what the works is all about. I know you've been locked up awhile and you have a few months to wait for my daughter so feel free to as you convicts say 'get your nuts out of pawn'," Chan said laughing as he was lead out of the room by two naked Chinese girls.

Two were left with Chris and they asked what he wanted because anything goes but he shook his head and said, "Just a full body massage". He couldn't picture himself with another woman but Lin and his mind was racing a mile a minute from what he had just learned from Chan. He would be making ten mil a month, damn! It was fixing to be on like a muthafuckcer for real! After the massage, Chris' mind was relaxed, and his body felt good. He was waiting in the car when Chan came out with four Chinese women hanging on his arms smiling. He gave each one a twenty-dollar tip. In return he got a kiss from each. He got in the car all smiles. "Ok Romeo, where to now?" Chris asked smiling.

"To the nearest gun store while we discuss other

problems," Chan answered.

"Problems? What do you mean, problems?" Chris asked.

"I mean like what's up with this so-called Mexican Mafia that you robbed. Are they a threat to you? Because if they are a threat to you, then they are a threat to my Lin and that's a threat to me," Chan answered.

"I don't know. They sent word to the jail when I was trying to make bond and said if I did get out, I was a dead man. But I didn't take it seriously cause if I had of gotten out, they got guns. I got guns too," Chris said.

"Well, I'm sending some of my people to this Mexican's house with the money that you took and let him know that we don't want any problems. If he chooses to step out of line after that, then I will erase him point blank," Chan stated. "Right now, we're going to get you some protection. I will still probably have to wait 72 hours while they check my background, but we will still have them in a few days."

They pulled up in front of the Greensboro Gun Rack and went inside. The owner was a fat redneck with a Budweiser beer gut and a tight ass Harley Davidson T-shirt on.

"Can I help you fellows?" he drawled as they walked to the front counter.

"Yes, I'm opening up a security company around here and this is one of my new students. I'm looking for some new weapons for my crew, so I chose you to be the lucky dealer that we purchase our guns from. My name is Chan Que. Here's my ID so you can go ahead and check my background."

"So, Chris, what kind of handguns are you used to

shooting?"

"I would like to see the 97 model Beretta 40cal., black, with the shoulder holster," Chris told the owner.

He went into the back room and came back with two of the prettiest 40 cals Chris had ever seen. Chris tried on the shoulder holster to adjust to his size. "Do you have any bullet proof vests in this place?" he asked.

"Yeah," the owner answered, "but it might be a little too rich for you your blood, boy."

"He aint't your boy and we pay cash on the spot!" Chan spit.

"Sorry sir, no offense intended," as he again went in back and came out with a black Teflon vest.

"We will take it all, the two 40 cals, the vest, the holster and I want that chrome pearl handled .380 too," Chan said pointing to the display case. "How long will we have to wait to get the guns cleared?"

"No time, sir. We have a new system that tells if you're a convicted felon and can't purchase firearms. You checked out clean, so you're good to go," the owner said. He boxed up all the merchandise and we left him with 'have a nice day'.

"So, what's next Mr. Chan," Chris asked.

"Well, we've taken care of everything in this state so what's the quickest route to Virginia from here?" Chan asked.

"Probably to take Hwy 40 to the 95 exit, follow that to either 158 or stay on 95 to Richmond, assuming that's where we're headed." Chris answered.

"Yes," Chan stated. "I want to show you where the dealership is located and introduce you to some of my people. But first we better stop at the Advance Auto and get a radar detector and then hit the highway for Richmond, VA." Along the way Chan made some calls on his cell phone and informed Chris that his people saw the Mexican drug dealer and he agreed to let by-gones be by-gones and was warned that if anything occurred, there would be repercussions to follow. He also said that his contact in the Governor's circle was checking on Lawrence Hilton's record and conviction and would get back to him before the day was out. Chris called his Mom and his sisters who were overjoyed that he was out. He would be back tomorrow around noon. He said hello to Lin and then got off the phone. He had things on his mind to discuss with Chan.

"Mr. Chan, is it because you are in the drug trade that you have problems with Lin becoming the first Korean Attorney General?" Chan just looked at him. "Yes, I saw the look pass over your face when she spoke of her dreams," Chris said.

"You are very observant," Chan said, "but you are right. I just don't want her to set her goals so high only to be crushed if something got out that her father was shipping drugs into the US. That's why you must do everything to protect yourself and us."

"I understand," Chris said. "Now to a better subject like what I'm supposed to do with the ten mill I keep a month. I mean, I want to help my family first because we've had a hard life, but I can't go and buy Mom Duke a crib. The feds would be on me in a second."

"You are correct," Chan answered. "That's where my people will come in. They have the skills to open new businesses to clean your money. As long as your family doesn't mind helping put it together, there shouldn't be any problems. But to get you started, I'm going to give you and Lin a million dollars as a wedding gift. Once I place it in a bank and pay the taxes on it. It will place your credit at the highest level and take some of the heat off you for a while until we get settled. If you want, I can have it wired into your account now and you can call your Mom back and tell her to quit her job," Chan stated.

"No, we can wait. I will have to see just what kind of ideas my family will have about opening new businesses that will make a profit," Chris said.

It was just about 5:00 pm as they took the exit into Henrico County. Chan used the car's GPS to find the Richmond Toyota dealership but first he and Chris stopped off at a barber shop to get cleaned up. Chris then drove them to the mall at Chan's request.

"I'm not trying to change you, but you are going to be President of this dealership. Even though your assistant will be doing all the real work, while you see to the shipments, you will still need to look somewhat professional., so I want you in a suit and tie when you come to the dealership. Once you leave, you can change back, ok?" Chan asked.

"I'm down," Chris said.

At the mall Chan picked out a silk suit by Armani, black silk shirt and grey silk jacket with matching grey slacks and a pair of black Gators. Chan gave Chris his platinum Rolex to complete the look. Chris got a pair of Sean John jeans, a Carolina *23 jersey and some new baby blue Jordans to wear back to his mother's house. From there they headed for the dealership.

"I must say that I do like the feel of these clothes. I might have to change my wardrobe," Chris joked.

"Yeah, just make sure you return my watch," Chan said, "it cost me $150,000."

"What?!" Chris hollered. "You got to be kidding!"

"Nope," Chan said, "that wasn't a joke."

They located the dealership and pulled into the front plaza. Chan pointed to the parking spot labeled 'President' and Chris laughed as he pulled the Porsche into the spot. He and Chan got out and checked out their surroundings. Chris was impressed. Not only was there some two hundred new Toyotas on the lot. The main building was a two-story glass structure. Chan explained that the company had its own bank and insurance companies right on the lot. They went inside the building and took the elevator to the top floor. Chris was even more impressed by the marble floors and oak wood desks. Chan went to the end office again labeled 'President' and pushed the door open. Inside was a spacious office with a desk bigger than the prison cell Chris had just left. To the right was a wet bar stacked with the latest liquors. To the left was an entertainment system with DVD and a 60-inch screen television. Everything was designed in dark blue marble with a blue carpet that felt like you were walking on snow.

"So, do you like?" Chan asked.

"Nice!" Chris said shaking his head.

"This is where you will conduct your business," Chan said. "If you must make any urgent calls, do so in here, especially if it's about our shipments, because that entertainment system is also a built-in jamming system for your cell phone and office phone. Just cut on the TV and no one can pick up your conversations. Your cell phone should be in your top, right side drawer. It also has a built-in scrambler; we can never be too careful." Chris walked around the desk and got the cell phone out of the top drawer. "This phone will be used to call Lin, me, your family, your associates and your assistants here at this company. Give no one else this number. If you have to talk to someone else, then use this office phone or get another cell phone," Chan stated. A knock at the door stopped the conversation as Chan answered, "Who is it?"

"It's Alexia, your second in command. May I enter?"

"Yes, of course," Chan answered.

Chris had seen beautiful women, but this blond-haired, blue eyed model was definitely in the top ten. "Alexia Davis, I want you to meet my future son-in-law, Chris Brandin. He is going to be our new President."

"It's a pleasure to meet you Chris," said Alexia, as they shook hands. "I'm looking forward to working with you. I take it that Mr. Chan has informed you of everything. Rest assured that I will handle all affairs of this company and you will be free to handle all of your affairs."

"Thank you, Ms. Davis," Chris said.

"Please call me Lexus," she said. "All my close friends do."

"Ok, Lexus," Chris said. "So, what do we do first, Mr. Chan?"

"We don't' do anything yet," Chan said. "All you do is be here for when the shipments arrive. Make sure the number is exact and that their destinations are correct.

Then, once you get the cash, give it to Lexus. She will deposit yours in a private, overseas account and do what she does best; wash the rest and get it to me."

"It's that simple?" Chris asked.

"No, nothing is that simple, but your part is mostly small," Chan said. "Like, for instance, our truck drivers have a high-risk job. They have to go through weigh stations and road checks but it's all covered because parts of the 18 wheeler have been removed to even out the weight and each truck is loaded down with 500 lbs. of C4 explosives so if shit hits the fan, the driver is instructed to run, then blow up the truck. No truck, no dope. No dope, no evidence," Chan smiled. "Once everything is settled and the first shipment of new Toyotas are on the way, you and Lexus can sit down and discuss everything," Chan said. "But right now, I'm starved so we are all going out for dinner and we are not going to discuss any business."

They had a nice dinner at a Chinese restaurant on Richmond's West side. They then went back to the dealership. Lexus had driven her 500 SL because the Porsche was a two-seater and they also had other business that needed attention.

"So, what's next on the menu?" Chris asked as Lexus pulled off in her candy apple red Benz.

"I need to make some more important calls so we can use your office and the scrambler for those," Chan said.

Back in Chris' office, Chan was on the phone talking non-stop in a language Chris hadn't yet begun to understand so he surfed the TV cable stations until he came to some new 50 Cent video on BET.

"That guy has become international because he stays on

our music stations in Korea," Chan said, getting off the phone. "I just spoke to my people and everything is ok on my end. They are just waiting for the green light. I also spoke to my Governor friend and he found something valuable on your friend Lawrence Hilton. He said he has an outstanding warrant in Queens police department for assault, inflicting serious injury which carries a maximum of six months. He's going to try and get his time terminated in NC and have him extradited back to New York, saying he has a more serious charge there. So, you need to write him and inform him of what's going on. Tell him to say he has a murder charge to face in Queens if anyone asks. Let him know that he won't have to do any more than six months for the assault but once he gets to New York, I will call a lawyer I know and try to get whoever he assaulted paid off to drop the charges."

Chris had taken a pad out of his desk drawer and was writing down everything Chan said. He left a note for Lexus to mail the letter to Pasquotank first thing in the morning.

"Ok, that takes care of everything for tonight so let's go get a room and get some rest so we can make it back to your Mom's house by noon," Chan said. "And, by the way, we get separate rooms because I might have some company over later."

"Ok, Romeo, that's cool with me," Chris answered. "All I want is a hot bath and to talk to Lin before I go to sleep."

"Oh, that reminds me," Chan said going in his pocket, pulling out a black velvet box. "This is for you. It belonged to my wife and I got it cleaned and re-sized so you can give it to Lin."

Chris opened the box and looked at the big 5 carat diamond with a platinum band inside. "It's beautiful, Mr. Chan. She must have meant the world to you," Chris said.

"She was my world, son. That's why there will never be another to have my love," Chan answered.

"I understand. I just wish I could've gotten the chance to meet her," Chris stated.

"Me too," Chan said. They both got separate rooms at the Meridian Inn. Chan went to his room and Chris went to call Lin and run a hot bath, his first in six years. After the water was run, he got his cell phone, stripped down, got into the water and called his Mom's house.

"Hello?"

"Hey ma, what you doing?" Chris asked.

"Nothing baby, just watching a movie off cable," she answered.

"It's too quiet for Nicole and Denise to still be there. They already gone?" Chris asked.

"Yeah, Nicole, Denise and Lin all went to the movies since Lin said she had never been to one in America. They should be back shortly. Are you alright?"

"Yeah, I'm just tired. Chan and I have been all over Richmond. He was showing me his business," Chris answered. "He wants me to help run his car dealership over here and help him find new places to open other dealerships. He also told me to ask my family if they have any business ideas to open new companies. He said he would back the ideas and my family could run them. So, start thinking of something you want to do cause you are quitting your job ASAP before we have our wedding. You can either help run some company or get your rest. Either way, your hard-working days are over."

"Oh Chris! This is truly a blessing from God. I always said to keep your faith and things would work out. But mostly I'm just glad you're home with your family and by the way, I really observed Lin today. You know your mother. But she's really a nice person. Even Nicole likes her, and you know how she is about your girlfriends. So, I think you made the right choice and I wish you both the best."

"Thanks, Ma. As long as I have your blessing, I'm alright," Chris said. "Do me a favor and call the bakery and order a birthday cake for Lin cause I want to celebrate with her and the family tomorrow. Her birthday is still a few weeks away, but I think the timing is right for tomorrow. Oh, before I forget, I got a new cell phone. The number is only for family. It's 553-8791. Give it to Nicole, Denise and Lin. Tell Lin to call me when she gets back. I'm going to finish my bath and lay down. I will see you tomorrow. I love you."

"I love you too baby. I'll see you tomorrow. Bye."

As Chris clicked off the phone and laid back in his hot bath, he knew he had made the right choice even though the game he had entered was very dangerous. He didn't care about the outcome as long as he took care of his family. He had dozed off when the cell phone interrupted his sleep, "Hello," he answered.

"Hi, my love," Lin said. "Did I wake you up?"

"Kinda. I just dozed off in the bathtub. Now I'm sitting here in cold water," Chris said getting out of the tub. "You have a nice time with my crazy sisters?"

"We had a ball," Lin answered. "They are a trip. We

went to see Matrix Four and I had a real nice time. That was my first movie in America."

"Where are my sisters anyway? Let me holla at them." "Well, you can't because they're gone. It was your Mom's idea to not tell them you were out until tomorrow and surprise them," Lin said. "They don't know everything about us yet. They think I'm a new friend of yours trying to get to know the family. They are going to be here tomorrow at noon so make sure you make it before twelve. That is, if my father will let you. I know how he is on the business subject. By the way, where is he anyway?"

"Oh, we got separate rooms cause he had other business to tend to," Chris said feeling uncomfortable.

"Yeah, he probably got some woman over there right now," Lin laughed.

"Well, if he does it only means that he's human and a man," Chris said. "What are you up to?" he asked.

"Your Mom and I are watching another movie, but I don't think I'm going to make it to the end cause I'm getting sleepy myself," Lin said.

"I'm going to turn in myself. I will be glad when I can turn in with you beside me," Chris said.

"Me too, Baby. You haven't been gone but a few hours and I miss you badly," Lin said, "so sleep tight and remember that I love you."

"I love you too," Chris said as Lin blew him a kiss through the phone. He clicked off, dried off and got into the bed with a smile on his face. With his new beautiful wife and Mr. Chan's connections, he was going to show all the niggas around his way how to stunt and them niggas from the G-unit ain't going to have shit on him. Chris and Chan got together the next morning and drove by the dealership to make a few more calls. Chris got in touch with his man from D.C., Anthony Boney (aka Yogi) and Rodney Frye (aka Lite) from out of Charlotte. They both would be down to check him out in a few weeks. He had left messages with Jermaine Foremans (aka Miami) and Big John Langford, a white dude out of Texas, to get back to him ASAP. Now all he needed was his main man, New York, to get free and it would be on and poppin'.

He wanted to call others from his family and let them know he was out, but Chan advised him that the less people knew, the better and besides, they would all be invited to the wedding. Chan called back to Korea and spoke with Myra to make sure everything was ok at home. She said someone called pertaining to CDJ and wanted him to call them when he had time. With all his business he had let CDJ slip his mind these days, so he decided to let Chris know what CDJ was before we hit the highway.

"I want to tell you about a sort of extended family of mine back in Korea," Chan said. "It's something that I hope we never have to use but I want you to know about it. Back about 20 years ago our military bombed what we thought was an abandoned building used by terrorists, but it turned out to be an orphanage for kids. Everybody inside was killed except three small girls in the basement. No one knew what to do so I adopted them and sent them to a Code of Justice school where they were taken care of and taught every step of martial art that the oriental race has to offer. They are what's known as CDJ, three women, all age 23, all beautiful and all cold-blooded assassins. Connie, Dominique and Jinx would lay down their life to protect me and my family because they honor me for raising and educating them. I'm telling you this because if you ever get into any drama and need help, that's who I would send. You might think, 'what good will three women do', but believe me, I've seen them in action They are perfect marksmen, trained with everything from knives to assault weapons and they are masters of Judo, Taekwondo and each have been through the legendary 36 Chambers,. All three can kill you with one motion of their bare hands and they have advantage over most men because they are beautiful women who will flirt and smile in your face one second and kill you the next," Chan said. "I'm dead serious so don't hesitate to ask for their help, especially if Lin's life is in danger cause they look at her as a sister.   Even if she doesn't know them personally, they know everything about her. Every time she went out alone, they were around her watching her and she never knew. That's how good they are."

"Well, like you said, I hope we never have a situation where we need them," Chris said.

"Me too," Chan said. "Right now, let's hit the road so we can make our lunch date at your Mom's."

Chapter 16

Chris had a good time at his Mom's house for lunch. His sisters were so happy to see him. Chan told Lin that he had deposited a million dollars in an account for their wedding present. Chris thought his Mom's and sisters' eyes would pop out of their heads.

"I've had a real nice time today. I feel that my daughter, Lin, has a real family in the US so I won't' worry so much while I'm back in Korea," Chan said.

"No," Chris stood and said, "I have a surprise for my Lin. Ma, if you don't mind."

His mother left and went into the kitchen. She returned in a minute carrying a strawberry shortcake with eighteen candles on top. They sang 'Happy Birthday' to Lin as tears of joy ran down her cheeks. Once she had blown out the candles and made her wish, Chris grabbed her hands and kneeled in front of her. "Baby, I love you, now and forever and I can't wait until you're my wife," he said as he slipped her mother's wedding ring on her finger. When Lin looked at it more tears dropped from her face.

"Oh, Chris! I haven't seen this ring for years. I was wondering what my father had done with it. It's so beautiful and yes, I love you too and can't wait to be yours always." They hugged as his Mom and sisters wiped their eyes as well.

"I hate to leave so soon but Lin and I have to be back in D.C. to visit the college she's to enroll in soon. Then we must go to Georgetown district to check on the house Lin picked out," Chan said. "But before I leave, I want to invite your entire family to the wedding, Chris.

Whenever the date is set, I will personally fly everyone down to Hawaii to attend, all expenses paid. Just get their names and get them to me ahead of time."

"I appreciate that Mr. Chan," Chris said as his Mom and sisters were silent with their mouths open.

"You use the Porsche until yours comes in and we will take the limo back to D.C. Meet me tomorrow at the dealership so we can put the final touches on our plans."

"That's a bet" Chris said.

After everyone left, Chris found his Mom in the living room sitting on the sofa in the dark. "Why you sitting here in the dark, Ma?" he asked.

"I was just thinking about you. Come in her and sit with me." He sat down beside his Mom as she took his hand. "Baby boy, you have been blessed beyond reasons. You've been released from prison, found a beautiful wife and given the opportunity to better yourself through her father. All I ask is that you give thanks to God and no matter how much money you come by, never forget Him and where you come from, ok baby?"

"You know I won't, Momma," Chris said. "I'm just glad I will be able to take the load off you. You deserve some rest and relaxation and you're going to get it. So, let me handle all the money problems from here on out. You just find ways to spend it."

"Ok, baby, but there's another problem we have to face," she said.

"What's that?" Chris asked.

"That's your Momma getting on an airplane. I told you I would never fly but there's no way I will miss my only son's wedding. So, I guess before we fly, we are going to have to smoke one of them blunts things you be talking 'bout."

"I guess so then," Chris said as they laughed.

 "I love you, my son," she said smiling.

Part II East Coast Takeover

Chapter 17

As Chris stood at Norfolk Regional airport waiting for his man New York to arrive he thought back to his conversation with Chan earlier. Chris had made Chan change his plans about the shipment of the dope. Instead of all five trucks coming to Richmond, VA, only three would come. The other two would go to the new Toyota dealership in Manhattan, NY. He would let his man, New York, handle the Miami and NY connects and he would deal with Charlotte, Maryland and Texas. That was his own way of showing loyalty to New York. They had started their bids together, went to war together and hustled together in prison. They had held each other down. Now this was Chris' way of holding New York and his family down.

"What's up my nigga!" New York screamed, ignoring the stares from others. He gave Chris some dap and put him in a semi bearhug.

"What's good baby? I told you I wouldn't forget my fam, nigga," Chris said. "I know you glad to be out of that concrete box my nigga, word up. What did they do once they transferred you back to New York?"

"Shit son, I had to stay on the island for a week. Got to see some old fam and shit but then they came and said the charges had been dropped." New York smiled. "So, what we got on the agenda for today?" he asked.

"Well, first we going to smoke us a blunt of some the dro. Get in the car, we going back to the dealership in Richmond and wait on the others to come in later today. Then we going to get down to business and lock this fucking East coast down my nigga!"

Chapter 18

Chris hit the blunt and passed it to New York. They were in the conference room across from his office in Richmond. He looked into the faces of the five men seated beside and across from him, assembling the words he was about to say.

"All of you have one thing in common. You know me, we've done time in one place or another. I feel that you are real and about your business or you wouldn't be here in the first place. All of us have hustled one way or another, whether big or small. We know the game. We are new in the big leagues and that means each and every one of us has to think and stay on point with the business at hand and the ones working under us. Your connect is me. My connect is a ghost. Point blank. Your job is to make money, move product and protect me. Here is the plan. You each will be given a job with the Toyota company in your area. You don't need any skills. All you need to do is dress nice come to work and let your Vice President handle all affairs of the company. Your job will be spreading the product. All money except your cut will be given to your Vice President, no questions asked. Now to the big business. Each dealership will get a shipment of new Toyotas each month. On this truck will be 100 keys of pure heroin. Each key is retailed at $100,000 apiece, no cuts, no shorts. So, your pickup should be ten million. You are to give your Vice President nine million every month. One million is for yourself. We have people that will help you wash your money and set up accounts. New York will handle NY and Miami to take some load off us here in Virginia. So, Meth, you got the dealership in Miami; you deal straight with New York. Everybody else will deal straight with me. That means Lite, Yogi and Big John deal directly with the dealership. Now I need to know; can everyone move the amount of product that will be coming into them?" All the men nodded. "Ok, any questions?"

Big John leaned forward, "Yeah, will we have to send our people to drive the trucks or will they come to us?"

"Naw," Chris answered. "They will all come to you. Once the three trucks arrive here, they will be sent separate ways to Texas, Maryland and Charlotte. Once they unload, they will come back here. Same as with New York. Two trucks will go to New York, then one will go on to Miami from there.

"I got a question," Yogi said. "What if you are left with some dope when the next shipment arrives?"

"Then that means you ain't got the clientele you said you had to get the product moved," Chris answered. "How much you think you going to be short, Yogi?"

"About 20 bricks," he answered.

"Ok, get with me later. I got a couple of homies out of VA that might need some work. I will holla at them and see what's up. Any more questions? Good. Oh, but one more important thing, don't hesitate to call if you get into any trouble especially with the jakes. If the police or worse, Feds, come anywhere near your dealerships, it's over. We shut your shop down and find a man to replace you. You take a vacation to Paris or somewhere. Now enough of business. Let's blow this joint and hit the club."

"Yeah, nigga, you got to get it all out of your system, fo' you get married," New York said laughing.

Chapter 19

The day of the first shipment everything was in order. Chris was in his office watching videos trying not to be nervous. He had called everyone three times already. Everything and everyone was in place. The phone rang. He jumped and answered it on the first ring.

"Hello. What's up Lexus? The trucks are here! Ok, I'll be right down." Chris started out of his office, then stopped and went back to his desk. He took his key and opened the bottom drawer and took out his 40 Cal and put it in his shoulder holster under his suit coat. He took the elevator down to the showroom floor. Outside of the glass showroom, he saw the four 18 wheelers parked beside one another. 'Four?' He thought, 'What the hell! It's only supposed to be three.' He walked through the doors leading outside with a slight frown on his face. Lexus saw his face and automatically came to his side.

"What's wrong, Chris?" she asked.

"Why are there four trucks instead of three? I thought we explained that only three were to come here." Chris answered. Lexus let out a sigh of relief.

"Oh, that. No baby, the trucks are right. Only three have product on them; the fourth has our new Toyota Spyders on it for our showroom. I'm sorry. I was supposed to let you know. That's my fault."

"It's ok," Chris said. "You've been there for me a lot here lately. I do appreciate all the work you've put in for me. If you ever need my help, just ask. Now let me go tell these drivers their destinations and give Mr. Chan a call and let him know everything's in order."

Chris walked over to the truck drivers standing by their trucks and asked, "Who has the truck with our showroom cars on it?"

"I do," said a small Chinese man stepping forward.

"Ok, you pull your truck around back and the guys from the garage area will help unload the cars. Then see Ms. Davis for your check." The Chinese man bowed and left for his truck. The next driver was Mexican. "You speak English amigo?"

"Si," he answered.

"You are to take this truck to Upper Marlboro, Maryland. It's a dealership on West 25th Street. They are expecting you. Any questions?" He shook his head 'no'. "Safe trip," Chris said as the Mexican left. The third driver was a 300 lb. redneck. "You know how to reach the dealership in Dallas, Texas?"

"Yep," he answered and spit tobacco juice on the pavement, some of which splashed on Chris' Gators.

"You seem to have an attitude. Anything me or my friend can do to help?" Chris asked, putting his hand on the butt of his 40 Cal under his jacket. The redneck didn't miss the move.

"No, no," he stuttered. "I'll be on my way." The last driver was another Chinese man who was smiling, having overheard the exchange with the redneck, when Chris stepped to him.

"Your trip is to East charlotte. The dealership's on Freedom Drive. Any questions?"

"None," he said, bowed and was off. Chris went back inside and took the elevator back to his office. Once inside, he cut on the TV and called Chan.

"Mr. Chan," he said, to sound business like. "Everything's in order. We got our shipment of new Toyotas for our showroom. I shall call you back once I've heard from the other dealerships."

"Alright, thank you Chris," Chan answered. "Now would you like to speak to Lin?"

"Yes, of course," he said. Lin had gone back to Korea to spend time with Myra, Chan and her friend, Niki, before she started college in 3 months. He missed her badly.

"Hey Boo!" Lin said.

"What's up, Baby girl! I miss you so much," he told her. "I can't wait to have you in my arms again." They still hadn't made love wanting to wait until their honeymoon, the first night after they were married. Chris had been out of prison four months and hadn't had sex with but only one woman. That was Lexus whom he worked with. They both understood he was to be married and so it was just sex between them.

"You been working hard at the dealership, Baby?"

"A lil' bit cause we got our first shipment of new cars today, so it's been a long day and I still have to wait to hear from all the other dealers," Chris answered.

"Well, at least it will keep you busy and away from the women," she teased.

The phone flashed on another line so he told her he would call her later and answered the other line. It was Lexus.

"I'll be right up," she said and hung up. "I wanted to let you know that fat, redneck truck driver reported to me saying you threatened him with a gun. I told him that he did right and that I would see to it that your black ass was fired," she said smiling. "Going to be hard to fire my boss though."

"Thanks Lex," Chris said. "But I don't want him driving anymore of our trucks."

"That will be handled on our Texas end," she said. "I already phoned in his termination right before I called you."

"Thanks again," Chris said.

"Yeah, but you've been a naughty boy," she said going over and locking his office door. "You can't be going around pulling your gun out on everybody. You know that, right?" she said, coming around behind his desk, "except, of course, on me. You can always pull your gun on me," she said unzipping his pants. Before he could say anything, she had him fully in her mouth. His toes curled as she deep throated him again and again.

"Damn, Lexus, you trying to fuck up a nigga's head?" he asked as he released in her mouth.

Once she had swallowed every drop, she said, "No, I'm just trying to relieve your stress until you're married away. Then you're on your own," she said heading for the door. Then she stopped and turned around and said, "You know, if your heart didn't already belong to Chan's daughter, I could fall for you hard. You know that?"

"Yes, I do," Chris said and then she left.

Chapter 20

Two months later

Chris sat in his office going over inventory. Then he stopped, looking around as if seeing everything for the first time. He still couldn't believe how his life had changed in just six months. He had made Chan a cool 70 million. He himself had 20 million of his own money in overseas accounts. His Mom had quit work. She, his two sisters and a cousin had opened two beauty salons and a night club. He and Lin had a nice two-story, six-bedroom, brick house in Georgetown and were to be married in a few weeks. All his people had moved product as planned and locked down the entire East coast, setting themselves and their families on higher grounds. He and New York had a banging new club in Brooklyn and New York was doing good holding his end down. As he was thinking all of this, his mother's voice popped into his head. At once he closed his eyes and spoke to God.

'Father, please watch over me and my family. Forgive me for my sins. I know it's wrong for me to be selling the stuff I sell but I promise to stop once my family is secure. I know that even though I've been so blessed with good fortune these last few months, the hard times are bound to come. Please give me the strength to weather the storm and make the right choices. Amen.'

Chapter 21
Columbia, South America

Tony Santiago's blood red eyes looked into the faces of the men sitting around the conference table at his mansion in Columbia. It was so quiet that it seemed as if everyone was holding their breath, which some actually were. "Damn it!!" He slammed his fist down on the table as they all jumped. "So! What you dick heads are trying to tell me is someone has managed in just a few months to cut all our sales off from the East coast? There haven't been any raids or any busts, so I know we haven't lost any product to the police. So, what the fuck is going on in Miami?" Benny was Santiago's main supplier out of Miami. He swallowed nervously and licked his lips.

"Tony, it seems that someone else is supplying Miami and other parts of the East coast with a purer grain of China White," he said. "Last month you sent over 50 bricks of uncut heroin at retail of 75,00 apiece. As of today, we still have 40 bricks left unsold that we can't seem to move. The ten that we did get rid of went into the Cuban neighborhoods so basically our own people bought them. All my other connects that I called said they were straight; didn't need any product."

"What?" Santiago screamed.

"They said they don't' need any product when we been supplying these niggas and wetbacks for years? That's bullshit! What I want you to do when you get the fuck back to Miami is get that crew of yours, go find one, any one of our old customers and find out who they are getting their new product from! I don't care if you got to cut his dick and legs off to get the truth. You find me a name ASAP!!"

"Yes sir," Benny replied, heading for the door.

"This meeting is over." Santiago said, leaving the room. He couldn't believe anyone could have that much product that could shut him down. Who? The Mexicans, another Columbian? He didn't know but he was going to call in some high favors to find out who had taken over his turf and they would pay dearly with their lives. Santiago took the stairs down into his basement to use his secure phone. He had a good friend high up in the FBI that had a nose for good product. He owed Tony some favors form the past when he was a field agent and now was the time to call them in. He dialed the Washington number.

"Hello. FBI Headquarters in Washington, D.C. How may I help you?"

"Yes, I need to be put in contact with regional director, Dean Hanks. It's a matter of great concern," Santiago stated.

"Please hold," the operator said. Tony Santiago bet they would be surprised to know they had one of the biggest suppliers of drugs to the US on the phone. He smiled at the joke. Then the smile disappeared when he remembered the reason for the call. He realized he just might not be the top supplier anymore.

"Hello. Director Hanks speaking. How may I help you?"

"Are you on a secure line?"

"Yes, yes," Hanks answered, recognizing the voice on

the other end. Dean Hanks had been a field agent assigned to customs in Miami when he met Tony Santiago. After developing a friendship through payoffs and free product Hanks would let Tony's product through customs only making small busts set up by Tony to make it look as if he was on his job. Tony Santiago was part of the reason Agent Hanks got his promotion and relocation to D.C.

"It's been a while Mr. White. How are you?" Hanks asked.

"Not too good," Tony answered, "and that's my reason for calling. I need a favor from you, really, just a lil information."

"Ok," Hanks said.

"First, are you or your department aware of any new suppliers along the East coast or West coast because I'm having problems with my company on my end. Sales are down big time so that means you've got a new player out there. And that's bad for me and you, understand?"

"I understand Mr. White but we only have a small development down in Dallas that should be handled shortly. If any useful information comes from that I will be sure to pass it on. I will put my contacts straight on it and get back to you as soon as I hear something," Hanks said.

"I appreciate that Mr. Hanks. I will be awaiting your call. Please check your drop mail in a few days. There will be something for your troubles," Tony said, hanging up.

Chapter 22

Seventy-two hours later Tony had all the news he needed. Benny and his crew had kidnapped and tortured a Mexican dealer. The man had given the location of a Toyota dealership out of Miami, Florida selling weight but didn't give any names. He said the product was coming in through another dealership out of New York. Tony called Agent Hanks back about this information. Hanks informed him all the new Toyota dealerships got their cars through the Norfolk shipyard; the main office being a dealership in Richmond, VA. His contacts couldn't tie any drugs to the dealership but another dealership down in Texas was being linked to major deals in that area. Undercovers were on the scene but so far, no arrests had been made. The last valuable piece of information Hanks gave Tony was that the dealerships in Miami, New York, Texas and Richmond were all owned by a Korean businessman named Chan Que. Santiago snatched up the phone. "Benny! Listen, and listen good. I want three crews put together ASAP. I've got a good feeling that we got chink behind these dealerships pushing major product on our turf. I remember my father used to talk about how the Chinese had major product over there, so I want the Miami dealership, New York dealership and the one down South in Richmond, Virginia hit and hit hard!"

"What's the target?" Benny asked.

"There are no targets. Tell the crew to spray the whole place. We don't know who is in charge or who's doing what, but I want to turn the heat up on these places so this way we send our message loud and clear to the one in charge. I want this taken care of in the next week,"

Tony said.

"Yes sir," Benny answered as the phone clicked in his ear.

Chapter 23

The last week of Chris' life had been like a fairytale. Chan had used his company jet and flown Chris and his entire family to Hawaii for Lin's and his wedding. He had rented the beach front as the scene of the wedding including having the group Jagged Edge sing "Let's Get Married". Most of Chris' aunts and uncles who could take off from work were there along with Myra, Niki and New York and his family. His sisters and Niki were the bridesmaids and New York served as the best man. Everybody had a ball dancing and partying, even his Mom who was scared to death of airplanes. After the vows were exchanged and pictures taken, Chris and Lin left for their honeymoon suite. Everyone else left soon to fly back home. For 3 days Chris and Lin had barely left their room getting to know each other's bodies. He looked down at his beautiful wife's face lying on the pillow beside him. She was his everything. He had enjoyed her body from head to toe, taking his time teaching her all the ways of making love. One thing he knew for sure was that his player days were over. He was her first and she was his last; the last and only woman he would be with. Now he knew how Chan felt about her mother when he said, 'there would never be another woman for him'. They were to catch a plane back to JFK later that day but right now all he wanted was to hold his wife again. As he slid his arms around her and pulled her tight, she moaned, 'I love you'. "I love you too Baby girl," he whispered, kissing her forehead as he closed his eyes and drifted off to sleep.

Chapter 24
Dallas, Texas

"Subject pulling out of the dealership now," Agent Bennet said into his walkie-talkie. He pulled his government issued sedan out to follow a few cars behind the Silverado truck. Two more agents joined in the parade, following in other undercover vehicles. "Subject turning off to Hwy 280 eastbound," Agent Bennett repeated as he entered the four-lane highway.

"Regular license check roadblock half a mile up," one of the agents replied. "

Ok, that's our pick-up. As soon as he stops, we converge. Make sure one of us is in front of his truck and one behind. I'm out," Bennet said. Agent Dunn shot by in an old Ford pickup to get in front of the subject. The subject was Donnie McCollum, aka Cowboy. He had sold some pretty pure heroin to an undercover DEA agent last week and they were trying to catch him dirty and link him to the dealership. If they could turn him, then they would have enough to go at Big John Langford and then at whomever supplies him. That was the plan but first they had small fish to catch. Donnie McCollum, aka Cowboy, had just purchased a half of key of heroin from his buddy Big John. He was a street-smart hustler who watches his surroundings when he isn't high on dope and today, he was wasted off two uncut lines of heroin, therefore he wasn't paying attention when he stopped at the checkpoint. He was straight. He had a license and no warrants so there was no reason for them to fuck with him or search his truck. He handed the trooper his license smiling until the trooper told him to step out of his truck. "For what?" Cowboy asked.

"I just need you to step out of your vehicle please," the trooper asked, his hand resting on the butt of his gun.

"What the fuck is this, some new kind of reverse racial profiling?" he asked.

"Sir, I'm asking you nicely to please step out of your vehicle!" Now Cowboy was suddenly very sober. He noticed the other troopers standing at attention and a plain clothes standing beside his car through his rearview mirror. Fuck! Something was up. Only one chance, he thought opening his door and stepping out. He hoped he still had his old high school track speed. As he broke into a run between the two trooper cars, he hit the medium and shot across the oncoming traffic in the other lanes. A car slammed on brakes to avoid hitting him as he hit the woods full speed. He heard a crash, then another louder crash as darkness engulfed him. At first, he didn't hear anymore sounds; then he heard feet coming before him, getting closer. He held his breath. The he heard a low moan that turned into a deep growl before his mind registered 'K9!' The dog was on him tearing into his legs like they were steel. Then lights came from everywhere. Police were yelling, "Lay down! Lay down!" so he laid down. It was over just like that. His lil' run was over.

Chapter 25
Miami, Florida

"Hello, this is Candy Freeman, Vice-President of Toyota, Inc. How can I help you?"

"Candy, this is Meth. I'm on my way to the dealership. You want something to eat?"

"Yeah, stop and get me a steak salad from Outback," Candy answered.

"Ok, I got you. I'll be there in about 20 minutes. Out." Candy hung up the phone and went across the hall to the restroom. She was just washing her hands when it sounded like a small war started somewhere outside. Out of reflex she fell to the floor. She had grown up on the south side of Richmond, so gunshots were nothing out of the ordinary for her, but she could hear people screaming and gunfire constantly coming. She closed her eyes and prayed to God for her safety. That's the way the responding police found her; on the restroom floor, eyes closed, lips moving silently. Meth had just gotten in the Benz coupe. He put Candy's salad in the passenger seat and pulled off into the street. He was about two blocks from the dealership when he noticed police and ambulances screaming by. 'What the fuck going on up here,' he wondered. His pulse jumped as he came to the dealership parking lot and saw that all the police and ambulances were in the Toyota parking lot! 'What the fuck!' As he switched lanes and turned into the bottom of the parking lot, he was stopped by an officer putting up crime scene yellow tape.

"Sorry, but you need to turn that car around," the officer said.

"I work here," Meth leaned out the window and hollered. "I'm the President of this company."

"Oh, I'm sorry sir but please pull off to the side. Everything from this tape up to the dealership is a crime scene. The homicide detectives will probably want to speak with you. They are up by the showroom." 'Homicide! What the hell!' Meth wondered. As he parked his Benz off in the grass and started towards the showroom. He froze now, really seeing what had happened at the dealership. All the showroom windows were shot out. The new cars inside the showroom were riddled with holes. Some 10 or 20 cars were shot up in the parking lot. He counted three, six, seven bodies on the ground with sheets over them. As he walked toward the showroom entrance, he saw two officers pulling sheets over Ken and Mike's bodies. They were his two top salesmen that worked the showroom area. He swallowed the lump forming in his throat. Candy! Where was Candy during all of this? He started towards the elevator when a tall, white guy stepped in front of him and flashed a detective badge.

"What's your business here?" he asked.

"I work here. I'm President of this dealership," Meth answered.

"What's your name?" the detective asked. "Jermaine Foreman."

"Why weren't you at work at the time of the shooting?"

"I was getting lunch for my Vice President. It's in the front seat of my Benz parked down in the grass," Meth stated. "Where is Candy? Is she alright?"

"Ms. Freeman is up in her office with a detective."

"Can I speak to her?" Meth asked.

"I guess," the detective answered "but just one more question before you go. Do you know any reason four armed men would want to shoot up this car dealership?"

"No," Meth answered.

"Have you fired or repossessed anyone's cars lately?"

"No, not that I recall. I'm sure that information can be found in the finance department. Now, can I see Candy?" Meth asked. When he stepped off the elevator he was once again stopped by a cop.

"Are you Mr. Foreman?" the cop asked.

"Yes," Meth answered. Then he was allowed to go by.

When he walked through her office door, Candy was on the sofa with a tissue in her hand speaking to another detective. When she saw him, she jumped up and ran into his arms. "You, ok, Candy?" he asked. She shook her head 'yes'. "Ok, good." He hugged her again and whispered in ear, "answer their questions as best you can, then go home. After I've spoken to our people, I will call you later, ok?" She nodded again. He started for the door, then turned and asked her, "I guess you won't be needing the steak salad in my car, right?" She smiled and shook her head 'no'. Good, he wanted to at least get a smile out of her. He managed to dodge the detective and made it back to his car. He knew Chris was probably still on his honeymoon, so he tried New York's cell number but got no answer. 'Damn it!' He had to wait to speak with Chris or New York to let them know what was going on but until then he would take his precautions. He headed back to his condo to get his guns and vest.

Chapter 26
Manhattan, New York

New York had just dropped off his son at his baby's mother's house. He had taken his lil' man out to the fair in New Jersey City for getting good grades in school. Now he was on the way to the dealership in Manhattan. He had some calls to make but he never took his company cell phone when he was with his son so not to be interrupted. He pushed his 500 SL, big body Benz through the streets of Manhattan thinking how happy his dawg, Chris, looked at the wedding they had attended in Hawaii. Even in the pen, Chris had always pulled the c/o bitches and had them open, bringing dope and money, but from what look he saw on Chris' face at the wedding, he knew the player days were gone. He was happy for him. Without Chris' connects, he knew he would still be in the beast, not out here eating like a king and getting to see his son grow up. He owed Chris his life and would hold him down no matter what cause real niggas were hard to come by nowadays. He had planned on stopping at his crib and changing clothes before he went to the dealership to take off the uncomfortable vest he always wore when he was in the streets, but he would swing by his place after he checked in at the dealership. He pulled in happy to see the people checking out the rides even though it was a front. He still got paid top salary for playing company CEO. He pulled into his parking spot beside the showroom. He hesitated whether he should leave his 357 in its stash box or take it up to his office. He finally decided to leave it be until he got to his place. As soon as he opened his door and his

Durango boots hit the pavement, the hairs on his neck and arms stood on end. New York froze looking from left to right. He didn't see the danger his sixth sense had alerted him to, as soon as his guard started to drop, two black on black BMW 745 Is pulled in front of the showroom window. Before he could move or blink, the side window dropped, and a masked face popped out of the sunroof with an AK47 in their hands. He felt an invisible hand jerk his right arm back as he ducked and darted for the office door. As soon as he got to the glass door, what felt like two bricks slammed into his back, sent him thorough the plate glass window. His last thoughts were of his son and other family members as blackness engulfed his thoughts.

Chapter 27

Georgetown

Chris and Lin had just walked into their house, coming from the airport. Chris was dead tired from the long flight, but he had to go to the dealership and pick up his cell phone and make sure things were straight at the other dealerships. Lin said she was tired also and was going to call her Papa ad then take a nap. Chris gave her a kiss and promised to be back before dinner. He jumped in his 911 and headed out for Richmond. It was about an hour drive to the dealership from D.C. As he pushed the 911 through its gears, he looked at the platinum, iced-out wedding band on his left hand, gripping the wheel. It was time to start planning for his future. Did he want the street life, knowing he had a family now to lose? Now that the East coast routes were in order, he could easily find someone else loyal to run it for him and Chan. He would have to have a sit-down with Chan on his next trip over and discuss their future. He also had to check in with Mom Duke. The hair salons and the club were bringing a profit in Greensboro. She had gotten a new house in Reidsville and bought a new Lexus 300 and a BMW M3 for his lil' sister, Nicole, and he bought his oldest sister, Denise, an H3 Hummer for her belated wedding present. She had married while he was in prison. Now that his main family were secure, it was time to build on his new family, Lin and himself. Lin wanted kids even though she had a lot of years left in college to get her degree in criminology. She could always take time off to have kids and then pick up where she left off the next semester at Georgetown. Chris still had in the back of his mind an uneasy feeling that everything was going too good and the bad times were right around the corner. He figured he would always be paranoid because in prison sometimes that saved your life. He automatically went in his stash box. He had gotten it custom made under the driver's seat to hold his guns. It was no more than a cash register drawer that locked or unlocked at the push of a button, but it was built into the seat so if searched by police, it would look like part of the seat. He hit the button and the drawer slid open between his legs. He pulled out his 40 cal while stopping at a light. He checked the clip and slid it in his shoulder holster along with an extra clip. He was just entering Henrico County, so he slowed down to about 45 mph because he didn't need to get pulled with his heat on him. He came up on the dealership through the back way by the garage area. He blew the horn at his head mechanic, Bobby, and waved him over. Bobby was an ex-convict out of Petersburg, VA and otherwise would've been still out looking for good work but Chris had hired him for two reasons. One, he was loyal and kept his mouth shut and two, he was a hell of a mechanic.

"What's up Pres?" Bobby said, calling him by the nickname he had given Chris short for President.

"Ain't nothing Bee," Chris answered. "I got a 911 supercharger coming in from overseas today or tomorrow. Think you can get her in without any problems?"

"I can handle it," Bobby answered.

"And I got a $500 tip if it's in before 24 hours are up," Chris stated.

"I got you for sure, soon as it hits even if it's Sunday, it's done" he said.

"Appreciate it," Chris said as he drove around the side of the showroom.

As soon as Lexus saw him pull up, she smiled and came out to meet him. "Your line in your office has been ringing off the hook," she was saying. He was getting out of his car, half listening to her, half looking at the car lot behind her. That's when he noticed two black Yukons pull up in front of the showroom window. That's when everything slowed down, and all hell broke loose! He saw two masked men jump out of the back of each SUV with AK47s, but things still didn't register until he heard them let off and bullets and glass started flying everywhere. He grabbed Lexus as bullets slammed into the car in front of them and his Porsche behind them. He didn't know if they tripped or what, but he and Lexus were thrown to the pavement at the back of the Porsche. He told Lexus to stay down, as his hand found the butt of his 40 cal. He could see sparks and glass flying, hear people yelling and screaming! The gunfire had turned in his direction, so he crawled around the back of the car parked in front of them and peeped around the back bumper. A masked gunman was walking towards where he and Lexus had fallen. He clicked off the safety, took a deep breath and came up firing the 40 cal as fast as he could pull the trigger! The gunman was caught off guard, not expecting the return fire. He hesitated a second before swinging the AK in Chris' direction. That second cost him his last breath. Three hollow point, 40 cal bullets hit his chest, throat and forehead, knocking him off his feet. The two other gunmen, thinking their work was done, ran back toward the SUV. But the last one, seeing his comrade go down, turned his gun in Chris' direction. Chris found himself looking straight into the hell of the AK. He dropped to the ground as the gun spit flames in his direction. He rolled once again around the bumper of a car's body. Chris was looking from under the car's bumper when he saw the gunman advance toward the car. Something he'd once seen in a movie flashed in his mind. He aimed at the gunman's boot and squeezed off two rounds. He was rewarded when the gunman screamed and dropped to his knees. Chris then fired again, blowing the man's kneecap apart. The gunman screamed again and dropped the AK47. Chris then realized that everything had gotten quiet except for tires spinning as the SUVs sped away. Thinking the second gunman he shot was dead also, his thought jumped to Lexus!! He pushed himself off the pavement and on shaky legs, ran back around to the Porsche and stopped in his tracks. The 40 cal he was holding dropped to the pavement. Lexus was lying by the back tire of his Porsche, eyes still open, hair spread out on the pavement. Blood covered her suit and the pavement under her body. Chris was frozen. He remembered her sweet laugh, the way she used to stare at him when they first met, the way she always handled business and took control of things around the dealership. Those pretty blue eyes. All these things flashed through his mind as one lone tear slid down his face. He dropped to his knees beside her, closed her eyes with his hand and kissed her forehead and whispered, "Rest in peace," hoping her departing soul could hear his words.

"Help! Somebody call an ambulance! Please! Somebody!" The screaming snapped Chris out of his state of shock. He picked up the 40 cal and walked around to see the wounded gunman lying on his back bleeding from his knees and feet. The man looked up to see Chris coming and automatically went silent. Chris walked up and stood over the gunman.

"Please! Please! Please man, don't' kill me! I got kids man, please let me live!"

"Take the mask off, piece of shit!" Chris barked. The man complied and Chris was looking into the face of a Mexican or a Cuban man. Thoughts of the Mexican he had robbed flashed through his mind, along with the guilt of putting Lexus in harm's way. "Now, listen and you listen good. You got about three or four minutes before this place is swarming with cops. Either you answer my questions and I say you were an innocent bystander, looking at a car and got caught in crossfire or you don't and you wear the charges for this shooting and I know for sure you got at least one murder charge from the body I just left beside my car," Chris stated. "Now, why did you do this? Who sent you to shoot up this dealership?" he asked.

"I don't know who gave the orders, man I swear! But I heard that someone here was selling heroin on the Cuban's turf, so our orders were to send a message. I swear that's all I know," the man said. Chris looked around the dealership. He could hear sirens coming in the distance.

"So, you say you were only supposed to send a message, right?"

"Yes, man, I swear that's all!"

"Well, send this one back then!" Chris screamed as he shot the man in the chest three times! "That's for Lexus! Motherfucker!" He walked over to the showroom. Luckily no one was inside due to the lunch hour, but he could see a man's body in between two bullet-riddled Toyotas. 'Damn! Just an innocent bystander looking at a car! Damn!', Chris thought. Then it hit him. 'Damn I just murdered a man and still got the gun on me and I'm an ex-convict. Oh shit!" He ran back over to Lexus' body, hearing the sirens real close now. He grabbed her hand and put it around the gun, pointed it in the air and pulled the trigger twice. Then he dropped it by the Porsche's front tire as he ran to the elevator. Once in his office, he took off his shoulder holster and took it to Alexis' office and put it in her bottom drawer. Then he went back and called 911 and reported the shooting, saying only that he was a concerned citizen, hearing gun shots. He got his cell phone out of his drawer and saw his voicemail was full. He turned on the TV and dialed Chan. He answered on the first ring. "Chan! Listen!"

"No, Chris, you listen! The dealerships in Miami and New York have been hit by drive-bys. I've found out it's some Columbian Cartel saying we are taking their sales," Chan said. "Get out of there, go home and stay with Lin until I call."

"But, Chan! They hit here too," Chris said.

"What!?" Chan answered.

"That's what I was calling to say. They just hit here. Chan, they hit Lexus' she's dead!" Chris stated.

"Go home or as soon as you can after talking to the police. I'm sending CDJ to stay with Lin until things smooth over," Chan said. "And Chris, I hate to tell you this now, but man, New York got hit in Manhattan. He's alive but I don't know his condition. He's at Brooklyn Memorial. Right now, my main concern is my daughter and you! So, call me as soon as you get home! I will call

Lin and let her know you will be there shortly and that
you're alright, ok?"

Chapter 28

"Ok, Mr. Brandin, tell me what happened again, then you may leave as long as you come to the precinct and give an official statement in the morning," Detective Begal stated.

"I had just pulled up after getting back from my honeymoon," Chris started. "I pulled up in my parking space and Alexis came out to meet me. She was saying something about my calls when, behind her, I saw four gunmen jump out with guns. She drew her gun and told me to get down. We were in between a company car and my Porsche. The gunman saw us, so he started to advance in our direction, firing. Alexis got him first, but his partner must have hit her. She fell beside me and handed the pistol to me. Another gunman came around the car, I guess thinking we were both hit. He pointed the gun at me. But I guess it was empty or jammed because it just clicked. I fired at him maybe five or six times, I don't remember. Then, after I heard the SUVs leave and the firing stop, I dropped the gun and crawled to where Alexis was, but she was already gone. I closed her eyes, kissed her forehead and came to my office and dialed 911."

"Do you know of anyone who would want to shoot up this dealership?"

"No."

"Do all your employees wear guns?" the detective asked.

"No, but Alexis also ran a security firm for Mr. Chan, so I guess you can check that out with him," Chris answered.

"Where is Mr. Chan?"

"I have no idea at this moment," Chris answered.

"Ok, but if he calls or contacts you, please have him call me," he said, giving Chris one of his cards.

"Yes sir," Chris answered as they walked to the elevator. Downstairs, Chris walked through a showroom that was now full of bullet holes and glass. He got the keys to a new Toyota Spyder and hit the highway back to Georgetown. He had a lot of calls to make but couldn't do it driving with his mind going a mile a minute and his nerves on edge, so he could wait until he got home.

Chapter 29

As soon as he pulled into his driveway, Lin came running out of the house into his arms. "Oh, baby! You ok?" she asked, tears running down her face.

"Yeah, baby, I'm alright, just a little shaken, that's all, but don't cry. We're going to be alright," Chris answered.

"Papa called and told me everything. I feel so bad about Alexis. He said he was sending some Korean sisters, Connie, Dominque, and Jinx to stay with me until he finds out who is shooting up his dealerships."

"That sounds like a good idea," Chris said. "I know they trained in everything and will protect you with their lives. I would feel more comfortable leaving you with them. When are they due in?" he asked.

"Papa said sometime early tomorrow. Their flight from Korea leaves in about two hours."

"Ok, baby, I need you to call the dealership and ask for mechanic, Bobby, in the garage area. Tell him once the police finish their business, have my Porsche towed to the Exotic Cars Dealership on Hillard Rd. Tell him to order everything fixed and I want bulletproof windows installed too. I will be in the study making some other very important calls." He went to his study and thought of who he wanted to call first. He had to get in touch with everyone, even the ones who weren't hit, to put them and their people on point. He grabbed his cell and punched numbers in as fast as his fingers would move. "Hello, hello? Who is this?" Chris asked.

"Who is this?" the female voice on the line responded. I'm calling to check on a friend of mine. New...I mean,

Lawrence Hilton. This is his homie from VA Chris."

"Oh, Chris, I'm sorry, this is his mother. I've been answering his cell all day cause some people calling just to be nosy."

"So, Miss Hilton, how is he? Is he going to be alright?"
"Yes, baby," she answered. "But only because he had one of those vests on. He got hit in his right arm and got some stitches in his hands and forehead from falling through a glass window. Besides being very sore, he will make it."

"Please tell him as soon as he feels up to it, to call my cell and tell him I'm glad he's alright," Chris said.

"I will tell him. Right now, he's sleeping form the pain medicine but as soon as he wakes, I'll tell him and, Chris, you be safe too, ok? I know about everything you did for my son and it's appreciated."

"Ok Miss Hilton, thanks," he said, clicking off. Damn, he was glad his nigga alright. He could focus a lil better now on the problem at hand. He hit his cell button again.

"Hello!" Meth answered on the first ring.

"Meth, what's up my nigga, I heard you got some heat down your way," Chris asked.

"Fo show! My nigga! Some niggas come through and wet the whole dealership. They merked like seven, eight people, plus my two showroom salesmen, but Candy and me straight. But what the fuck going on Cee!"

"Check it, some Cubans from down your way seem to think we selling on their turfs. I got that from a gunman that hit us who wasn't so lucky."

"What! You got hit too my nigga? Why didn't you say something?"

"Yeah, they sprayed us and New York too, so it was a devised plan. The bastards killed my VP, Alexis. But I merked two of them bitches before they got away. One was wounded. That's how I got the information. He said a message was to be sent to us, so I sent him to hell with a message!" Chris laughed. "But I want you to lay low, keep the dealership closed for now cause the police going to be hot. Once the Feds see the connections, they going to swarm." Chris said. "So, you just chill, take a vacation or something, you and Candy, cause I know she got you open anyway, so give her my regards too and I'll get back at you."

"You sure, my nigga?" Meth asked, "cause me and my niggas can load up and come down that piece strapped."

"Naw, I'm straight. Right now, we just need to lay low until my peeps can holla at who trying to start this war. Feel me?"

"Ok, be safe my nigga, one," Meth said hanging up. Chris clicked off and hit the buttons again.

"The deal?" someone answered. "Get Yogi, Cee on the phone. It's a damn emergency!"

"Ok, my bad, hold one," the voice said. Chris heard the person banging on a door and Yogi hollering,

"What the fuck you want?! Cee! What's up my Nigga? What's wrong?" Yogi asked a few seconds later out of breath.

"Listen my nigga, some Cubans done hit our dealership in VA, New York and Miami sending a threat about we slanging on their turf, taking their sales. They just jumped out and sprayed everything in sight," Chris told him.

"What the fuck! You want me to load up the guns and get them Northeast boys and come see you or what? They want war, we can give them war!" Yogi barked.

"Naw my nigga, the police hot on the set right now. I'm just calling to put you on point. I want you to close the dealership and lay low until I hear back from my peeps, ok?"

"Bet my nigga, just let me know what's up soon as you can and if you need me, just call." Yogi said.

"One," Chris said as he cut the line. Two more calls and he could chill and wait to hear back from Chan

"Hello? What' up Lite?"

"Ain't shit lil bro, just maintaining out here in the Queen City."

Chris ran down to him what happened and advised him to close the dealership until he heard back from him. He then made his last call to Texas.

"Howdy," Big John answered.

"Big Jay, this Chris. You somewhere we can talk?"

"Hold on. Ok. Yeah, what's up Cee?"

"Some Cubans pulled a drive-by on our lots in Richmond, New York and Miami, talking about we on their turf so we shutting down until further notice. I will get back to you soon as I hear something," Chris said.

"Ok, but how long you want me to stay closed?" Big John asked.

"Until I hear back from my peeps," Chris answered.

"Ok, I get you."

"Ok. I got you. I'm gone." Chris said as he hung up.

Big John hung up with Chris and went back into his bedroom with the two women he was with. One blonde was pushing a needle into her arm with her eyes closed while the other redhead waited her turn. Big John had been keeping one or two keys of uncut heroin for himself and his personal use. He had been using the dealership to make more money on the side after cutting the dope. He had a big customer coming by the dealership tomorrow. He wasn't going to close up now and miss that money, but Chris didn't have to know that. He laid back between the two women and closed his eyes as the needle slid into his vein.

Chapter 30

Tony Santiago's phone woke him up at quarter to three in the morning. "Hello?" he whispered into the phone.

"Mr. White, how are you? I'm sorry for the time but I wanted to update you on our situation," Agent Hanks said.

"Yeah, alright. What's happened?" Tony asked.

"From what my agents are reporting, all dealerships owned by Mr. Chan Que are shut down as of right now except one in Dallas, Texas. Which happens to be good luck for us because yesterday agents arrested a small time, local dealer by the name of Donnie McCollum with a key of 65% pure heroin. He has confessed to buying it from one John Langford, aka Big John. That's the President of the Texas dealership. We've set up an undercover buy for tomorrow. Since everything moves through the Richmond dealership, I did some checking on the staff there. Seems the President of that dealership just got released from prison six months ago. I figured he was the connection, so I dug a little deeper and come to find out all the dealership presidents have prior felony records. But the biggest information came from our overseas office in Hawaii. Seems Mr. Chan's daughter married a few weeks back on the beaches of Hawaii and surprise, surprise! Who did she marry? None other than Mr. Christopher Brandin himself! So, you see the connection I'm sure. The Richmond dealership was a target of a massive shooting yesterday in which the vice-president, Alexis Davis and a few by-standers were killed. Chris Brandin was unharmed. He killed one of the gunmen in what was ruled self-defense," Hanks stated. "I hope you will find this information useful. I will let you know how things develop in the Texas setup. The guy, Donnie McCollum, doesn't know who supplies John Langford but if we can get Big John to tie in Brandin, then we can put him away for life on conspiracy to traffic heroin across state lines. I will keep you informed," Hanks said.

"Thank you, Mr. Hanks. You've been a lot of help. Please check your mail in 24 hours," Santiago said as he hung up. Tony laid back in his king-sized bed, staring at the ceiling. So, this Chris Brandin had married Mr. Chan's daughter and was the connection to the dealerships moving dope in on his turf. Tony had taken over the business after his father retired. Other members of the cartel had said he lacked heart to make the right decisions to bring money to Columbia. He couldn't let this Chink take over his turf because it would look bad in the cartel's eyes and disrespect his father's image. So, he had to move fast and hard. He rolled over and got his black phone out of his night table. He found the number he was looking for written in red. It was written in code only he could understand. He dialed the number.

"Ellow," a foreign voice answered!

"No Face. One-six-zero," Tony stated and left his cell number and hung up. Five minutes later his cell phone rang.

"Hello? Hi, Mr. Santiago. Nice to hear from you again. How can I help you?" the voice asked.

"I have a target, or rather two targets I want eliminated. Location, US East coast. Subject's name is Chris Brandin and I want his wife also. Can you handle it?" Santiago asked.

"Of course," the man answered. "Two million cash: put it out with your garbage tonight."

"Safe hunting," Santiago said as he hung up. He had dealt with the man called No Face once before. He knew his reputation. No one had ever seen the man's face. He moved as a ghost and changed his codes after every hit. He always got his target. The two million was a good investment; only pennies to Tony Santiago. He would hit Chan where it hurt; take away his daughter and most important, his son-in-law, his only connection to the East coast.

Chapter 31

Chan sat in his living room with all the lights dimmed, sipping straight Vodka. His mind was racing with different thoughts after hearing from his contacts inside the government import/export trade. He had found out who his enemy was. A Columbian cartel member by the name of Tony Santiago had ordered hits on the car dealerships because of declined sales of their heroin coming out of Columbia, but that wasn't what had him stressed. What had him stressed was he had also found out Tony Santiago was the son of Phillipe (Poppa) Santiago, a retired drug lord from Columbia and also his dead wife's father. So that meant Tony Santiago and his late wife, Lynn Richardson, were half-brother and sister by different mothers. He hadn't spoken to Poppa Santiago since Lynn's death because he blamed the war and his daughter's death on Chan and Korea. He always sent his granddaughter, Lin, birthday and Christmas cards full of money which Chan always returned to him. He always said he wouldn't bring his dangerous lifestyle around his grandbaby, but now with Lin's and Chris' lives in danger, he had to contact Poppa Santiago and have him talk to his son to see if things could be worked out. He didn't know if Tony knew Lin was his niece, so to speak, but that was the only way of trying to bring peace between the two. Chan looked at the number written on the pad beside his phone. He thought of all the pain he went through losing his wife. He knew he couldn't let that happen to his daughter. He took a deep breath and dialed the number.

Chapter 32
South Villa, Columbia

Poppa Santiago was just making his last lap in his pool when his cell phone rang. He swam to the steps and grabbed a towel from a pool chair to dry off. He grabbed the phone and sat down under an umbrella to shield the sun. "Hello," he answered with his thick accent.

"Poppa Santiago, it's been a long time. How are you?" Chan asked. The silence on the phone lasted a long couple of seconds.

"What can I do for you, Chan?" His tone was not friendly and dead serious. "Is my granddaughter alright?" he asked.

"Yes, yes, she's fine," Chan answered as he heard Poppa Santiago exhale a sigh of relief. "We need to discuss some serious business between our two families. Are you on a secure line?"

"No, but if you give me about two minutes, you can call back on my red phone," Poppa answered.

"Ok," Chan said as he wrote down the number given to him and hung up. Poppa Santiago entered his villa and told his main servant to pour a straight shot of Tequila and bring it to his study. He went upstairs to his room, got out of his swimming trunks and put on a fresh, dry pair of Safari shorts and a shirt to match. He was just entering his study when his red phone rang. He pressed a button on the side of the phone to scramble the call. "Are we secure now," Chan asked.

"Yes, of course," Poppa answered.

"Listen, Poppa Santiago, I know we haven't spoken in almost 15 years and you blame me for things that I had no control over, but I want you to know that I lost my soul when I lost Lynn. I would give up my life to trade places and bring her back. Right now, I need you to listen and put our past differences aside. There are some things I need to inform you about concerning my business and my (our) family. Since Lynn's death I had to find ways to prosper for my family. I bought into an import/export car ownership when it went bankrupt. With luck and good business deals, we turned the company around and now we have major dealerships all over the Eastern United States."

"Sounds like you made a good business choice," Poppa Santiago stated.

"Yes," Chan answered, "but it was all set up as a front."

"A front?" Poppa asked.

"Yes, a front; something I'm sure you are very familiar with or were before you retired." Poppa's eyes got big! "Yes, I'm saying we use the cars to ship drugs into the US – pure China White, 100%, no cut. As I said before, my soul died with Lynn. There will never be another, therefore I couldn't have a son to carry on my trade. I hadn't found anyone I could trust to move the company product into the US until my daughter met an ex-convict, fell in love and married him."

"What! Are you saying my one and only granddaughter has married and not one soul told me or thought to send me an invitation?" Poppa thundered!

"Calm down, Poppa. It was not a real big wedding," Chan lied, "and that is the least of our problems at hand."

"Well, damn it, what is the problem then?" Poppa snapped, still pissed about the wedding.

"The problem at hand is your son, my wife's half-brother has hit three of my dealerships with drive-by shootings killing two of my salesmen, a vice-president and about ten innocent by-standers."

"What the fuck! Why the fuck would my son, Tony do that?" Poppa screamed.

"Because he somehow found out we were moving product on the East coast, supposedly his turf. So, this was his way of sending a message to us. But I'm coming to you because my son-in-law Chris, was almost killed at one of the dealerships. He had just gotten back from his honeymoon with Lin, my daughter, your granddaughter. She was just dropped off at home. She could have been with him when he went to the dealership and what we could have had would be the same thing that took my beautiful wife, your daughter, from us. An innocent soul caught up in somebody else's war!" Chan breathed letting the words and realization set into Poppa Santiago.

"Damn that boy," Poppa barked. "These so-called thugs these days don't have any principles or honor. That's why I chose to step away from the trade. Chan, thank you for calling. I know we've had our differences in the past but at least you cared enough to call. What I can't figure out is why my son would bring heat on himself like that. He's not in the need for money so why not just focus on the West coast and the surrounding countries? Russia alone could make him a billionaire but then again, I already know the answer. I've seen it in his eyes before. I've felt it in my own heart at one time. Greed!" Poppa whispered. "Chan, I'm going to see my son today and have a sit down and make sure he understands everything. I know he doesn't know you and his half-sister were married because he was only a kid when she died. He definitely doesn't know about her having a daughter which in blood is his niece, because I chose not to tell him, but as of today, he will know everything. Give me your number and I will call you ASAP! One more thing before I go. Please consider taking your son-in-law out of the game he's in. Remember, I lived it for 30 years. It's dangerous especially to a man with a family out in the open. My granddaughter is all I have left of my daughter so please remove her from harm's way. That's all I ask."

"Yes, Poppa Santiago, I will do my best and have a talk with my son-in-law. Please ring me when you've spoken to your son."

"I will," Poppa said as he hung up. "Bella!" Poppa hollered to his maid. "Please have them bring the car around. I'm going to see my son!"

Tony's driveway and yard were packed with limos and all kinds of exotic cars when Poppa's limo pulled up. "Let me out here Paco," Poppa said as he got out at the end of his son's driveway. Poppa made his way around the cars instead of going in through the front door. He went around the side of the mansion. As he came upon Tony's pool, it was crowded with all kinds of people. Women were everywhere wearing less than nothing. Men were doing coke by the lines and chasing women here and there. Poppa turned and went inside to find his son, Tony, was in his conference room when Poppa walked in on him. Out of respect for the retired drug lord, everyone around the table stood. Tony glanced behind him and stood to address his father but before he could reply his father addressed the men. "Everyone, please leave me to my son." Without any questions asked, the room cleared.

"Father, is everything alright?" Tony asked, shocked at his father's face.

"No! I want to know why you sent out hits to the US without even considering notifying me. Tony, I've always preached to you about bringing unwanted heat to yourself and the cartel. Why did you do it? You have enough money for five lifetimes. What are you trying to be, some sort of TV gangsta?" Poppa asked.

"No, Poppa! I just want it to be known what parts of the US I control. I won't allow any product sold on my turf especially without my consent or my cut!" Tony stated.

"So, you have everything all figured out, right?" Poppa asked. "Well let me tell you something you don't know. First of all, my daughter, your half-sister, that was killed in Korea when you were a kid, had a daughter by her Korean husband. That child is my only granddaughter. Her name is Lin named after my daughter, Lynn, only spelled the Korean way. She just got married last week to a guy named Chris Brandin who runs the Toyota dealership in Richmond, VA; the one you put a hit on." Poppa looked at Tony watching the color drain from his face. He waited a minute to let the reality set in. "Chan Que married my daughter back when you were just a child. Until today, we hadn't spoken since Lynn was killed. He called me today and put all the cards on the table. Even though he's also in the heroin trade, his main concern is his daughter. Her husband, Chris had just arrived at the dealership when your goons hit. Luckily, he wasn't hurt but my grandchild could have been there and could have been killed all because you want to play big gangsta." Tony was silent, his face even more pale, sitting down in his chair not knowing what to say.

"Poppa, are you saying I have a niece and she's married to this guy, Chris Brandin?" Tony whispered. "If that's the case, then I'm so sorry because I've made a big mistake. Poppa, please forgive me," Tony asked as he took his father's hand.

"What, what is it?" Poppa asked sensing Tony had more to say.

"I... I put a hit on Chris Brandin and his wife ... my niece, to get back at Chan Que," Tony said.

"You did what?!!" Poppa exploded.

"I'm sorry, Poppa!" Tony said again as he put his head in his hands covering his face. Poppa Santiago grabbed Tony by the arm and pulled him up into his face.

"Tell me now, this moment, who you hired?!"

"No... No Face, Poppa. I hired No Face to kill them!" Tony cried to his father.

"Damn it! You stupid Fuck!!" Poppa roared as he went to Tony's phone. "Is this line secure?"

"Yes," Tony answered.

"You better do everything in your power to cancel that hit because if one hair on my granddaughter's head is harmed, you and No Face will sleep together!" Poppa spit as he dialed Chan's secure number. Tony, looking pale and scared, didn't know what to do. He knew once you hired No Face he wouldn't stop until the job was done. He also knew that No Face's phones and codes were changed after every job, so he had no way of contacting him. His father's voice brought him out of a daze. "Hello! Chan, listen carefully. My son has made the mistake of hiring a hit man to go after Chris and Lin. He is going to try and locate him to cancel it, but it might be too late. You need to get in touch with Lin and Chris and let them know, plus put protection on them," Poppa said.

"I already have," Chan answered. "I'm on my way to the airport now where my company jet will take me to Dulles in Washington. I will call ahead to Lin's and let them know. You can contact me on my cell or at this number." He gave Poppa Lin's home number.

"Ok, I will get back to you as soon as I know something and once this is all behind us, you, Tony, Chris and I will have a sit-down," Poppa said.

"I agree," Chan said as he hung up the phone and dialed his daughter's number.

"Yeah," Chris answered.

"Chris, this is Chan. Have you heard from CDJ yet?"

"Yeah, they are on the way from the airport now."

"Ok. Look, it seems that a Columbian has put a hit out on you and Lin to get back at me. So, once CDJ gets there, you let them know to be on the lookout and stay on point, all of you. I will be on my way there in a few hours. One more thing and this stays between us. You already know Lin's grandfather is Columbian. Well, it seems that this Columbian, Tony Santiago, is Lin's uncle or half-uncle. He and my late wife were half-brother and sister. He just found out today himself and is supposed to be trying to lift the hit, but it might be too late if the hit man's already left for the states. I just wanted you to know but Lin can't know out of respect for her grandfather."

"I understand, Chan. I will do everything in my power to help protect Lin. I will let CDJ know of the situation as soon as they arrive," Chris said.

"Ok, I will be there shortly. Be safe until then," Chan said and hung up.

Chapter 33

Chris sat in front of his 60-inch TV watching a movie, but his mind was in other places. He didn't like the idea of lying to Lin, but he understood why Chan would want to keep ger grandfather's name out of it. He knew anybody would have to kill him first to get to Lin, but to know that a hired hit man was coming at you and your family was something to put all his nerves on end. Chris went into his study and unlocked his bottom drawer of his desk and took out his Smith and Wesson chrome 45. If a hit man was coming, then he would be ready. He heard a horn blow outside and looked out to see a black limo pulling up. Good, he thought; now he had help in protecting his family. He had been looking forward to meeting the girls CDJ Chan spoke of so highly. He opened the front door as the limo driver came up with their bags.

"Where to?" he asked.

"Upstairs on the left. Any room," Chris answered. When he turned to look back at the limo, he was stunned. His wife, Lin, was an exotic beauty in a class of her own but these three Korean women were beautiful in their own way. They all had the smooth, creamy complexion and the dark, slanted eyes. Two were tall and the other one was shorter and muscular with her hair cut close. She was the first to greet Chris at the door.

"Hi, I'm Jinx," she said in perfect English. "You must be Chris? Nice to meet you," she said as she shook his hand with a surprising grip. The next two could have been twins because they were almost the same size and had the same features. They were Connie and

Dominique, not twins but sisters. Chris greeted them both as they entered the house. He told them Lin was upstairs resting and their rooms were upstairs on the left.

"Please make yourselves at home and comfortable cause we have some things to discuss when my wife wakes up," Chris said as they went upstairs.

Chapter 34

Chris, Lin Connie, Dominique and Jinx sat around the dinner table eating pizza. They had talked and gotten to know one another. Chris had let them, and Lin catch up on things going on back in Korea but now it was time to discuss safety. "Ok girls I hate to ruin your get together, but I have bad news that we need to discuss between us."

"What's wrong Baby?" Lin asked.

"Just listen Baby, because it's serious. I talked to your father again while you were resting. He called to inform me he had spoken to your grandfather and he found out who gave the order to shoot up the dealerships. Seems somebody told a Columbian drug dealer Chan was selling drugs through his dealerships. So, being that this was the Columbian's turf, he sent hits to each dealership."

"But Baby, why would someone lie on my father like that?" Lin asked.

"I don't know," Chris answered, but not before he caught the glances between CDJ. Good, he thought. At least they know what Chan really does for a living. "Anyway, that's still not the bad news. It seems that your grandfather found out that the Columbian hired a hit man to kill me and my wife to get back at Chan, so we must protect one another until they can get this straightened out and cancel the hit. Chan is on his way here as we speak, but what we will do is get prepared in case this hit man strikes. I'm told that you girls can handle your own. I have a few toys that I've collected in the basement safe. Take what you like and if there's something else you will need, just let me know." The girls all nodded their heads. "Any questions about anything?" Chris asked. Jinx raised her hand. "What's up?" Chris asked.

"Do you have a room in the basement also?"

"Yes," Chris answered.

"Then I think it would be wise for you and Lin to move there until this is over," Jinx said. "Hit men use sniper rifles and think of your bedroom windows."

"Good idea, Jinx. Anything else?"

"Yes," Connie spoke up. "Let's see your toys."

"Fo sho," Chris said as they all went down the stairs to the basement. Chris had gotten the basement fixed into a small game room. It had a large, marble pool table in the middle of the floor. To the right was a large, wrap-around sofa with a fold out bed. A 60-inch TV sat in the right corner by the wall. To the left was a small shower stall. Behind the pool table was a small refrigerator, a sink and oven. Chris had a small weight room over in another corner. Behind the weights was a small door. Chris went and hit the code on the alarm system and pulled the door open. He hit the light switch. Inside was made like a small walk-in closet but this closet didn't have clothes in it; only guns and more guns – all types, sizes and kinds on the shelves.

"I wondered why you kept this door secure so much," Lin said looking at Chris.

"Protection," he said and winked.

"Protection my ass. This is an armory!" she said. Connie, Dominique, and Jinx were like kids in a candy store. They had gone to pick their toys. Connie picked two twin 380s and a Mac II with shoulder straps.

Dominique got a .357 revolver and a street sweeper. Jinx, liking big guns, got two black on black Desert Eagles with the rubber grips and infrared beams. She also got a .30 .30 rifle with a high grain scope. They all were smiling like babies. "Well, at least my worries are solved," Lin said. "I thought you had all your porno tapes locked away in here," she said as they all laughed.

"You all straight?" Chris asked. When they came out, they all nodded. "One more thing," Chris added as he went inside and came back out with a bullet-proof vest. "Sorry Baby, but this is your second skin until this is over," he told Lin. "I have one upstairs in our closet that I will wear."

"Come on baby, I don't want that hot thing on," Lin snapped.

"It's only for when we moving through the house, baby. It won't be that long," Chris answered.

"Ok, but do I have to wear it to bed too?" she joked. "Hell naw, you know I ain't going for that," Chris said smiling as the girls laughed. "Ok, you are on ya own for a while. I need to make some more calls." He had been thinking about his homey, New York, all day. He decided to call and check on him in the hospital. He dialed New York's cell phone

"Yo! What up?" York answered.

"You, nigga, cause you ain't called and let a nigga know if you dead or what," Chris said.

"It ain't like that my nigga. I'm just now coming off them drugs. I been high as a muther fucker for real."

"So, what's the deal with your war wounds?" Chris asked.

"I'm straight so far. Got hit in my arm; shit went

straight through, but I'm sore as fuck. Got four bruised ribs where the vest stopped two of them, so I've been laid up for a while" New York said. "You find out where this shit came from?" he asked.

"Yeah, my nigga and it's crazy. A fucking soap opera," Chris said. He then told New York everything about Chan and Lin's grandfather and about the hit.

"My nigga, I'm supposed to be out of here in seven days, but I can leave early. I will be down there ASAP," New York said.

"Naw, my nigga. We straight. I got three soldiers staying with Lin and me. Some of Chan's friends. You just lay low and heal up," Chris said.

"Ok, my nigga but if shit get out of hand, don't hesitate to call. I'll bring some Queen Bridge goons down that piece and we will have war," York said.

"Word! But I will holler back when things settle down. You maintain and get well. One," Chris said hanging up.

Chapter 35

Big John had a hangover from hell after the party the night before. As he pulled into the dealership, he couldn't wait to get to his office and have a fix. He could feel the need deep in his bones. He got out and used his key to let himself in and took the elevator up to his office floor. It was a quarter to seven in the morning. His contact was supposed to be there at seven sharp. Plenty of time to have a good fix. He went to his desk and got out his works which consisted of a heavy-duty rubber band, a silver spoon and a needle. He took out his personal vial of heroin, shook a fix into the spoon, dropped a small amount of Vodka in it (that was his own specialty), then took his lighter and heated the spoon for about five minutes. He soon had a clear liquid in the spoon. He gently blew on it to cool it some. The he drew it into the shaft of the needle. The he tied the rubber band around his bicep to get a good vein to stand up. Once he found the vein with the needle, he pushed it in and injected the dope into his blood stream. Everything else was heaven to him.

Chapter 36
Dulles – Washington, D.C.

Chan had just gotten off the phone with Poppa Santiago again. Poppa had informed him about Tony's contacts inside the FBI and DEA. He said one of his dealers out of Texas was being set up to sell to an undercover agent early this morning. Chan had just arrived at Dulles Airport and had forgotten to set his watch. He had to call Chris and get him to call Big John in Texas to warn him. If the Feds got him, no telling what he might tell about the trucks and cars. He hurriedly dialed Chris' number. "Hello?" He heard a sleepy voice answer.

"Chris?"

"Yeah, this me. What's up Chan?" he asked.

"Listen, you must contact your friend in Texas. I've found out he has been set up by someone he is selling to on the side. He is to be set up by an undercover DEA officer early this morning. You must contact him now because the deal is supposed to go down this morning," Chan stated.

"Ok, I will get right on it," Chris answered coming fully awake.

"I just arrived at Dulles. I should be at the house in about 30 minutes. But this needs to be handled ASAP!" Chan stated.

"I'm on it," Chris said as they hung up.

Chapter 37
Dallas, Texas

Big John had gone down to meet the buyer. He was a white dude about 6'4", tattoos on both sleeves of his arms. He was driving a blue Lexus 400. "Nice ride," Big John said as he let the man in. He was carrying a briefcase and a cell phone. They took the elevator up to his office. "So, what do they call you?" Big John asked as they went into his office.

"Steve. Everybody calls me Steve."

"And how did you learn about me again?"

"Me, Donnie and Cowboy used to hang tight and he gave me your number," Steve answered.

"Ok, Steve. Let's see what you got in that briefcase?" Big John asked. Steve laid the briefcase down on his desk and opened it revealing stacks of money. "How much?" Big John asked.

"Two hundred thou," Steve answered. Big John went around and sat down at his desk. He was about to unlock his bottom drawer that contained two keys of uncut heroin but the sound of his cell phone ringing, stopped him. He grabbed it and answered.

"Yeah!"

"Big John, this is Chris. Are you alone?"

"No," he answered.

"Ok, then you listen carefully. My people just called and told me they got information from an inside source that the DEA had you set up to buy from an undercover this morning!" Big John looked up into the face of the man standing in front of him.

"Hold on a minute," he said.

"Steve, I know you're a busy man, probably in a hurry, but this is my wife bitchin'. But it won't take long so could you step in the hallway a minute."

"Excuse me," Big John said. "Ok, Chris, I appreciate this. I will find a way to get myself out of it."

"You do that," Chris said, "because you know you broke the rules by selling on the side, right? And I told you yesterday to shut that shit down, man."

"Yeah, I get you. I will call you later if they don't arrest me anyway, but you can believe they ain't getting no dope. No dope, no evidence. I'm out," Big John said as he hung up. He got up and walked out to the hallway smiling at Steve. "Sorry 'bout that. You know how women are about money. Bitch woke up and couldn't find any of the money I'd left for her and she went to bitchin'," he said as they both laughed. "Ok, back to business. We going to move this across the hall to the conference room, so you grab the money and after I get the product from the other office, I will be right over, cool?"

"That's cool," Steve said as he grabbed the money and went across the hall to the conference room. As soon as Big John saw his back turn, he went into his desk drawer and took out the two keys of heroin. As he came out of his office, he glanced in and saw Steve talking on his cell phone. 'Pig Bastard! Probably getting everyone in place.' Big John stopped at the restroom and flushed all the dope down the toilet. He wasn't going back to the pen, no way. He took a piss, washed his hands and went to address his friend Steve, the cop.

As soon as the man saw Big John enter the room, he got off the phone.

"Ok," Big John said calmly. "Here's the deal. You take the briefcase with the money in it and get the fuck out of my dealership!"

"What! What the hell is going on?"

"I'll tell you what's going on! You a fucking cop! Your cover's blown asshole, so quit playing games," Big John screamed. Steve stopped and looked at him, then took out his phone and called for backup. Then he pulled out his Glock and pointed it at Big John.

"You're under arrest, asshole, for conspiracy to sell deliver and traffic heroin."

"Yeah right," Big John said, "and if you find any drugs on these premises, I'll suck your dick." He could hear the other cops storming the dealership. "Oh, and one other thing, I want my lawyer present." Several other agents stormed in the room with a big, black guy wearing a Captain shield.

"My name is Captain Daniels of the DEA. You won't need your lawyer because we gonna talk first. And, what I ain't gonna do is bullshit you, just as you better not bullshit me," he said. "First," he said, sitting down beside Big John, "What I know? First, I know you've been moving drugs out of here to different parts of Houston, Mexico and Dallas. Second, I know you're a junky yourself, so if we don't happen to find anything here, what's in your system will stand up in court for the government. And, just so you know, we ain't going to let you off with that 'I'm an addicted junky' story. Nope, not after we got signed statements and a key of heroin off ya boy, Danny (aka Cowboy) McCollum. He's saying you the man, so we got you as the man around these parts. Out of the gate, we are shooting at 25 to life and that's just for the Kingpin status. Nothing less for Big John, right?" Captain Daniels said.

"Fuck you," Big John screamed.

"Ok, when we get thorough tearing up this place, we will see who gets the last laugh."

Two hours later, Big John's ass was sore from sitting handcuffed in the back. Two agents were with him while the others tore the place apart. Captain Daniels came strolling back in with a trash bag. "I told you I wouldn't bullshit you. So, this is what we got, about a quarter of a key out of your bathroom pipes. Don't look so amazed. What you didn't know is how long it takes that much dope to dissolve, especially when your pipes are backed up. You should have used liquid Drano," he said as the other cops laughed. "We also got a personal bottle of some pure shit out of your desk. I'm thinking that was your stash, and looking at your eyes, you need some now. Then we got a loaded 9-millimeter out of your office. You know that's a no-no by a convicted felon, but that's the least of your worries. Now, here is the biggest moment of your life. This answer will make you or break you. All we want is Mr. Chan and Mr. Brandin 'cause we know that's who's running these dealerships. Give us the details of how it's coming in. Work with me now cause if you turn me down, you won't get a second chance 'cause agents are picking Chris Brandin up as we speak. So, what's it going to be, big John?" You going to play with the big boys or you going to die in prison? Which one is it?" Captain Daniels asked. "Say 'yes' and today you go into our witness protection program. No time and a free mind.

That's my offer. So, what's it going to be?" he said looking down at Big John. Big Jon slightly nodded his head 'yes' to the Captain. "Jones, Dilworth, get him on a chopper now. Contact me when you get to your location. Let's tear this shit down to the ground."

Chapter 38
Georgetown

Chan and Chris sat in his living room later that morning. Chan had come in from the airport, greeted all the girls and pulled Chris in to discuss the hit. "I know you hate sitting around waiting like this, but we have no choice. To move around in the open would be taking a risk." Chris said. "I know. I just hate the thought of someone, anyone coming at my family, but one thing's for sho, he will have to go through hell to get to Lin and that's word on everything I love!"

"Excuse me," Jinx said, coming into the room, "but we have two dark colored sedans casing this area. They went by twice and now they have stopped down the street." Chris was already on his feet looking out the living room window. Now the two sedans had backed up and were coming down their driveway.

"Jinx, you go and let Connie and Dominique know what's up. You three cover Lin until we see what's up," Chris said.

"Ok," she said as she shot up the stairs. Chris was still looking out the window as four men in dark blue suits got out of the sedan and approached the front door. Chris signaled Chan to move to the other side of the door. Chris drew his 45. Chan had his 357 revolver out as a knock was heard at the door.

"Who is it?" Chris asked.

"FBI! We have a warrant for Chris Brandin's arrest!"

"Put some identification up to the peep hole," Chris requested. The two agents in front showed their badges. "Looks straight," Chris whispered to Chan. He handed Chan his gun and Chan left the room. Chris opened the door and the agents stepped inside.

"I'm Agent Smith and this is my partner, Agent Dixon. We have a federal warrant for Chris Brandin. Is that you?"

"Yeah," Chris answered.

"We have to take you to headquarters in Washington to face charges. Our Regional Director wants to question you. You have the right to remain silent and a right to have an attorney present." As Lin and Chan entered the room, they were placing cuffs on Chris.

Lin rushed and put her arms around his neck. "Baby, what's going on? What do they want?" Lin asked with tears in her eyes.

"I don't know, but I'll be alright. They have to take me to Washington," Chris said. "Chan, call our attorney and tell him to meet me at the FBI headquarters in DC. Lin, please get out this doorway and back in the house. I will call as soon as I know something," Chris said as he kissed his wife and left with the agents. Chan pulled Lin away from the open door and back into the house. "Don't cry sweetheart. Everything will be Ok. We will have him out as soon as we see what's happening. Right now, we still need to stay focused on your safety first. I'm going to call our company attorney and have him meet Chris in Washington. He will let me know what they have." Chan got on his cell phone. After making sure the lawyer would meet Chris, he also made a call to Poppa Santiago.

Chapter 39
FBI Headquarters – Washington, D.C.

Agent Hanks walked in the interrogation room where Chris and Agent Dixon were waiting. "Excuse us Agent Dixon," Hanks said as he sat down across from Chris. "I'm going to get right to the point to let you know we aren't here to pussy foot around or play games. So, here's what I know. I know Chan Que used his connects to get you out of prison early. I know he has fronts set up as car dealerships across the east coast to ship heroin in from Korea, and I know you set him up with his contacts in these different cities. Now…."

"Excuse me, but I know you're not trying to question my client without his lawyer present!" Chan's company lawyer said as he rushed into the interrogation room. "Jim Patrick Stenson and I represent Mr. Brandin. I hope you haven't tried to question my client."

"No sir, he was just telling me what he knows," Chris said smiling. The lawyer's cell phone rang, so he stepped away to take the call. Director Hanks leaned forward to whisper to Chris.

 "I also know that if you don't give Chan up, I'm going to personally see that you get 25 to life," he said, smiling.

"Is my client allowed to receive this call? It's his wife," Mr. Stenson asked Hanks.

"Yeah, go ahead. It might be awhile before they speak again," he said with a smile on his face. The lawyer handed the phone over to Chris.

"What's up baby?"

"Chris, this is Chan. Listen carefully. Director Hanks has

been on Tony Santiago's payroll for awhile and he has a nose that loves candy. Use it to your advantage. I think it should be enough to get him off your back. Tell the lawyer to call me back when he hears more."

"Ok baby, thank you and I love you," Chris said as he hung up feeling like a mountain was just lifted from his shoulders. He smiled at Director Hanks. The director smiled back at him. "Mr. Stenson, could you give me and Mr. Hanks a minute alone?" Chris asked.

"I don't think that would be a wise thing to do, Mr. Brandin," the lawyer answered.

"Please," Chris said, "I know what I'm doing. Just give us a minute."

"Ok, but I must warn you to watch what you say," the lawyer said leaving and shutting the door behind him.

"So," Director Hanks said smiling, "have you come to your senses and decided to help the FBI out?"

"Director Hanks, you've told me a lot of things you happen to know and guess what, everything you said is true," Chris said, and Hanks smiled yet again and sat forward in his seat. Chris leaned forward and looked directly into Hanks' eyes. "Now, let me tell you what I know. I know you a dirty pig. I know you've been on Tony Santiago's payroll since you were a field agent and I know you have a nose habit that likes good candy." Director Hanks had paled, his mouth hanging open like he couldn't breathe. "And last but not least, I know you better drop this investigation and these bitch ass charges on me and let me the fuck up outta here in 10 minutes or I will call my uncle Tony and tell him what a bad, bad boy you've been." Chris was still laughing as Director Hanks got up and shot out of the room like his hemorrhoids had flared up.

"What the hell did you say to him?' the lawyer asked, coming back in. "He looked like he saw a fucking ghost!"

"He just found out we have a lot in common," Chris said, grinning.

Director Hanks came back and told them they were free to leave. As Chris was walking off, Hanks stopped him. "Your problems ain't over like you think," he said. "you got major problems down in Texas. Tell Tony to call me ASAP."

Twenty minutes later, the lawyer and Chris were pulling up in front of his house in Georgetown.

"I appreciate you being there for me Mr. Stenson," Chris said. "Send the bill to my address and there will be a $500 tip for getting there so fast."

"Thanks, Mr. Brandin. "Please give my regards to Mr. Chan."

"I will," Chris said as he left the lawyer's Lincoln and walked to his front door. As soon as his hand touched the doorknob, the hair on his neck and arms stood on end. He spun around, looking across the lawn, both ways down the street. He knew he was being watched but he didn't see anyone. He quickly went inside and locked the door. Lin came running down the stairs and jumped in his arms.

"Oh baby, I'm so glad everything is alright. What did they want?" she asked. "Why did they have a warrant for you?"

"They asked me about the shooting, then about some gangs moving drugs, but in the end, the warrant was dropped. They just tried to scare me up," Chris said.

"Don't worry baby. I ain't going nowhere."

"I was so scared they were going to try and send you back to prison. I would have gone crazy," she said. He pulled away from her and looked into her eyes.

"Listen baby. I got a feeling that this hit man may be close by, so I want you and the girls to move to the basement for now," Chris said.

"Ok, and I will let Papa know you're back," she said going upstairs. Chan came down talking on his cell. Chris could tell by his face the news he was hearing wasn't good. 'Damn, what now,' he thought.

"Ok, thanks Tony. We will talk again soon," Chan said hanging up.

"By the way, Hanks said to tell Tony to call him," Chris said.

"That was Tony. He has already spoken to Director Hanks and it doesn't look too good down in Texas."

"What's going on down there?" Chris asked, but as Chan started to speak, Lin and CDJ came downstairs headed to the basement.

"Connie and Dominique, I need to speak with you a minute." They came over to the table and sat down with Chris and Chan. "Chris, the DEA got a guy named Donnie McCollum with a key of dope. He's the one that set up Big John. They got a quarter key out of the restroom pipes and a gun out of Big John's office. Word is they put pressure on him, and he broke. He is to testify in front of a federal grand jury in 72 hours. If he tells what he knows, all we can do is go back to Korea. We will never be able to set foot is the US again and I will lose my entire company, not including the charges your associates will face. So, we will have to move now and move fast. Chris, you, Jinx and I will have to watch Lin and the house because Dominique and Connie are going to Falls Spring, Idaho. Big John is being held there in a Motel 6. There's a small café a mile from the motel named Susie's Home Cookin. Two agents and Big John eat there every night between 8 and 9 pm. That's the only information we could get this fast. Girls, I've loved you like a father since I found you. This is by far the most dangerous situation we've been put in so far because there are so many risks, but my family's lives lay in your hands. So, go do what you were trained to do. Blend in and use all your skills. If it can be helped, don't kill any agents or cops unless it's totally necessary. But if you get the target and have to kill an agent get out as fast as possible. Call me and I will have the company jet waiting. Your flight leaves in 20 minutes. Once you're in Idaho, a car will be waiting for you. It will be your choice of what way you want to return and I'm sure that will depend on the heat you draw. Again, I love you both. Be safe," Chan said as both girls got up to get small traveling bags and catch a taxi to the airport.

Chris knew the danger was near. His sixth sense hadn't failed him yet, so he would be prepared when the person tried to hit. He and Chan had worked out a plan for the night. Chan would sleep upstairs and be armed while Chris would take the living room sofa. Just him and his 45. Lin and Jinx would have the basement. So, everything was settled. He wished he could smoke a blunt right now to settle his nerves, but he never smoked around Lin. He decided to go down and get a nice workout to relieve some stress and relax. While he worked out, Lin and Jinx watched a movie on the big screen. For some reason, Chris was still on edge even after the workout. He felt like everything was coming down. He couldn't believe Big John was working with the Feds after he had put him on and helped him and his family eat. The dude had been solid in prison but that goes to show that everything that looks solid ain't solid. He knew one thing for sure. After this, if they made it out alive and not locked the fuck up, changes were going to be made and that was a promise. But right now, they had to get through the night and Chris felt like it was going to be a long night, for real. He would protect his wife, by any means necessary. Win, lose or draw!

Chapter 40

No Face was directly across the street from Lin and Chris' house. He had broken into the house late last night after knocking on the front and back doors satisfied that it was vacant for the moment. He had taken up his surveillance from there only to be surprised the next morning by the cleaning maid. She was now in the deep freezer downstairs in the storage room. Before snapping her neck, he had gotten out of her that the owners, a retired couple, were gone to Canada for a month. Perfect. So, he could take his time. He would have taken Chris Brandin out in the driveway earlier. He had his high powered 50 caliber rifle scope directly on Chris' head from the time he left the car to the door, but he didn't want to alert the others inside the house. He had to get them together. Whomever else was in the house had to die also! He knew Chris, his wife and an Asian man were there. He had also glanced an Asian woman who he took for another maid, looking out the upstairs window. Then a few hours ago, two nice looking Asian women came out and jumped in a taxi and left. Yes, this job would have to get up close and personal. He dismantled his rifle and put it back in its case. Then he took out his two black 22's with the fitted silencers. He also had two stealth, steel hunting knives that would cut through bone. These were his specialties when up close and personal.

Chapter 41
Falls Spring, Idaho

"Fuck! This is some boring shit man! I need some dope. I need some pussy!" Big John said.

"Yeah, yeah, we know how it is John. Just hold on a few more days and you will have a new life, a new start," Agent Dixon said.

"What the fuck ever!" Big John said.

"At least you got your appetite back the other day," Agent Simpson said. "I thought you were going into DT's there for a minute. You had me worried about you."

"Fuck you. Worried about me? You ain't worried about my white ass! You just worried I might have died before I could have helped the government out, that's all," Big John said looking up as two fine ass Chinese bitches came in and sat down at the table facing Big John. "Look at these fine ass bitches out and about with no man. Damn, I need some ass bad. Ain't you got no government hookers on your payroll?" Big John asked. As the agents laughed Big John watched the two women order their food as they sat close to one another's ears sneaking peeks at him while laughing. Big John blew them a kiss and they just giggled. The agents ordered another round of coffee for themselves and a pitcher of beer for Big John. He had been thinking hard these last few hours about prison and what he had when he got out, nothing. Now he had two million in overseas accounts all thanks to Chris putting him on. The same man that he would testify against in a few days. Deep in his heart he feels this shit is wrong, but what can he do? He can't go back to prison. 25 years. Ain't no way. He's already 45 years old. He would be 70, no way, but to bring Chris down after he helped him get his Mom a house to have for herself to retire. Damn, if he could just give these agents the slip and get out of the country and to his money overseas, he could disappear. Fuck it. At least he could try. Fuck it. If they catch him, then he would go into the Program. Big John sat thinking and looking at the two women. They moved closer together. One leaned over and whispered in the other's ear. Then, to his disbelief, she stuck out her tongue and licked her friend's ear lobe. Big John sat frozen, staring over his glass of beer. The two women turned to one another and before he could think of what might happen, they kissed a long, passionate deep kiss that made him hard as a rock. Then they looked at him and giggled again. Damn, Big John thought to himself, 'if I could just dump these two jar heads and get with them. Shit, I would take them out of the country with me and have a fucking ball.' Between his hard-on and the two pitchers of beer, he had to piss. "Fuck, I got to piss!" Big John said, struggling out of his seat. Once he stood, Agent Dixon stood with him. "What? You going to come and hold my shit for me?" Big John asked.

"No, but I will escort you to make sure you get back safely," Agent Dixon answered.

"Whatever," Big John said, stalking off. Susie's Home Cookin was no more than two small rows of booths seating about 24 people with six bar stools at the counter. The bathroom stalls were down a small hallway in the back of the building. The men's door was first and the women's last. Big John and Agent Dixon went into the bathroom. Big John took a stall while

Agent Dixon used the johns against the far wall. As he was zipping his fly, Agent Dixon heard the door open and someone else enter the bathroom. He turned to find two Chinese women in the corner hugging and kissing as if they were in a hotel room instead of a public men's room. Big John came out of his stall and stopped dead in his tracks, smiling at the women. Agent Dixon cleared his voice as the women broke apart looking embarrassed.

"Oh, we sorry. We thought this was the women's," they said and giggled.

"It's ok girls. I kind of like to watch," Big John said as Agent Dixon made his way to the door. But, before he could register what was happening, one of the girls had chopped him in the windpipe. Damn, he couldn't breathe as things went slow. He felt another chop to the back of his head, then a kick to his face and he saw darkness and felt nothing else. Big John was so caught off guard by the women's actions that he couldn't even close his mouth. The two women walked toward him, running their hands over his body, feeling his chest, arms and legs. One kissed him in his open mouth and looked into his eyes.

"Mr. Chan doesn't like those who run their mouth," she said stepping to the side. Big John felt warm liquids run down his chin as the woman spit something on the floor. He still couldn't do or say anything.

The other woman whispered. "Bye, bye Big John." As he looked at her, she raised two 380's and put two shots in his head. Connie unscrewed the silencers and placed the guns back in her holsters. She and Dominique exited the men's bathroom hugging each other. They stopped at their table where Connie left a twenty. While the other agent sat reading a newspaper, the two women walked out into the fresh, Idaho night air. Back in the rental car, Connie started it and drove away.

"You one crazy bitch," she said to Dominique. "What you talking about, sis?"

"You know what the fuck I'm talking about. We sitting there putting on a show doing all this kissing and you got a fucking razor in your mouth. Bitch, you crazy! If you would've cut my mouth, I would beat your ass for real," Connie said, "but let's get going cause I'm more worried about Jinx and Lin.

"Right, let's get the fuck out of these boonies."

Chapter 42

Georgetown

No Face was dressed all in black. His face was painted with black war paint. He had cleaned his presence of the house across the street. Only the maid would be found in the freezer to prove someone had been there. He made his way across the street, staying in the shadows so not to be seen. He first cut the target's neighbor's phone line and power just in case someone happened to make it or see something from next door. He eased his way to the back of the target's house, cut their phone lines and power lines and tossed the wire cutters. His plan was to get to the second story ledge and enter the house through an upstairs window. He figured Chris and his wife slept in one of the upstairs rooms. He would hit them first, then the others, burn the house to the ground and disappear. He quietly stepped on the central air conditioner box and jumped to catch the bottom floor roof. He pulled himself up onto the roof, glad for his daily workout of pushups and pullups. He made his way around the house to the back-bedroom window. Once below the window, he made his way up to the second story ledge. He came to the upstairs windows and slipped his Teflon, steel knife out if it's case on his hip. Working silently as possible, he popped the lock on the window and slid into the house. As soon as the assassin's feet touched the floor in the other bedroom, Chan's eyes opened. He didn't know what had awakened him, but he sat up in the bed and looked at the clock. 12:00am. He was thirsty, so he decided to check on things and go down to get something to drink. He got out of the bed, slid on his bedroom slippers and went out into the hallway. He stopped at the head of the stairs, wondering why it was so dark in the house. Hadn't they left the upstairs light on? Then, like a flashing thought, he realized the clock beside his bed couldn't be right because he had gone to bed at quarter to one, so there was no way it could be 12:00am. He started to go back for his gun in the dresser drawer by the bed. Then he heard the door to one of the other rooms upstairs open. He turned back thinking it was one of the girls or Chris, just as two 22 bullets silently hit his chest. As he fell to the floor, he was still wondering what or who had hit him. Visions of his life flashed behind his eyelids. His last thought before blackness engulfed him were of his beautiful daughter, Lin.

In the basement, Jinx sat up from the sofa. She had heard a small noise from somewhere above. Probably Chris or Chan moving around using the bathroom or in the kitchen. Lin was cuddled up in some blankets on the floor. Jinx wished Connie and Dominique were here. Why hadn't they called or anything? Why was it so dark? She looked to see the time on the built-in VCR, but it was black too. She got up and made her way to the staircase in the dark. At the top of the stairs there was a little light coming from the living room window. As soon as she stepped into the room, a hand grabbed her around the mouth. She felt the cold steel of a blade pressed against her throat.

"Are the others downstairs?" No Face whispered. Frozen with fear, she didn't answer. "Answer me! Or you die!" She made a moaning sound behind his hand. As soon as he started to remove his hand Jinx turned her body to the left, put all her weight into her left leg and hit No Face with a sharp elbow to his kidneys. She knew there was a chance that her throat would be cut, but she was going out fighting, but the move had caught No Face by surprise. She felt the sting as he started to press the knife into her skin, so she dropped low. The knife caught the bottom of her chin. She felt it cut all the way to her jawbone, but the adrenaline kick in. She caught No Face in the jaw with another elbow and spun out of his grip. She felt blood running down her neck as she backed to the top of the stairs. No Face faked a swing with the knife and kicked Jinx in her chest, sending her back down the steps in the darkness. Lin jumped up off the floor when Jinx landed at the bottom of the steps.

At the same time, Chris was asleep on the sofa. He jumped as he heard something crash down the basement steps. He instantly grabbed for his .45 under the sofa cushion. As he stood up, he froze. He thought he was looking at a shadow by the stairs until the knife in No Face's hand caught the light coming through the window. "What the fuck!?" Chris said as he raised his .45 and fired at the shadow. The first hollow point hit No Face high in his left shoulder and spun him around. The second shot hit the wall behind him. As he dropped to the floor, he pulled his 22's out and let loose a silent flurry. The glass flowers on the table behind Chris' head exploded, glass pitchers and candle holders shattered on the table in front of him. Only then did he realize the shadow was firing back with silencers. Chris dove behind a leather chair and rolled into the kitchen. Downstairs, Lin ran over to see Jinx lying on her side dazed and bleeding. She grabbed her under the shoulders and pulled her over to the sofa. Then she ran and got a towel and wiped some of the blood away from Jinx's face. There was a deep cut along her jaw line and a lump beginning to darken on her forehead. Once Jinx's eyes focused, she shook her head and sat up in pain. They both had heard the gunfire from upstairs. Now they looked at each other as things had gone quiet.

"Lin, get those two Desert Eagles for me and keep the .357 revolver. If you don't hear these babies go off when I get up there, then shoot whomever shows at the top of those stair."

"But what about Papa and Chris?" Lin asked.

"Listen!" Jinx said grabbing her arm. "If I don't call down to you and you don't hear these guns bark, then chances are, they are both already dead." Lin shook her head as tears ran down her face.

"Are you sure you're ok?" She asked wiping away the tears.

"No, I hurt like shit, but I'll make it," Jinx said as she started slowly up the stairs.

Chris was still on his knees in the kitchen. He was worried about Lin, Chan and the girls. Why was it so quiet? No one could've slept through all that gunfire. He didn't want to think that they were all dead. He remembered the crash that had awakened him. Then he started to get pissed. Fuck this! He wasn't going to sit back and let some mother fucker terrorize his house. Hit man or not, this was his shit and if Lin was dead, he would make this bastard pay for real or die trying! He crawled around the counter and dove behind an end chair. More bullets tore into the wall behind him. He needed to make it to the closet behind the sofa. He slid across the floor and pulled the door open quickly, falling into the closet. More bullets hit the outside of the door as he caught his breath. He searched in the dark, pulling down a rack of clothes and some of Lin's furs until he found what he was looking for – his Teflon vest. On his knees, he laid his gun down and pulled the vest on and strapped it in. Jinx was almost at the top of the stairs when she heard more glass breaking. A silencer, she thought, as she backed down a few steps to regroup. Her face was tight and swollen and her head hurt like shit, but she was trained to ignore pain. The other shots had to be Mr. Chan or Chris. That meant that she had to be extra careful in the dark, especially if everyone had their guns out. She didn't want to walk into an already dangerous situation and end up getting hit by friendly fire. She looked back up to the small light at the top of the stairs and started to back up. Chris, still on his knees in the closet, thought about his life, Lin and Chan. He loved his wife more than anything. He had never believed in love at first sight until that day in the prison visitation room. He owed Mr. Chan his life for getting him out of prison and putting him on his payroll.

So, this was it. He had already stashed twenty million in an offshore account and written a last will and testament that left everything to his Mom and sisters, so at least they would be straight. He had run the streets since age 14 packing guns, selling drugs and running with straight killers, so he wasn't afraid of any hit man. If this was his day to die, then fuck it. He would go out blazin. He stood up, bowed his head and closed his eyes. "God forgive me for my sins and accept me into thy kingdom," he said, then he kicked the closet door open and charged into the living room.

No Face was still on his knees behind a chair in front of the basement stairwell. He got off the floor and pressed his hand to his shoulder to stop the bleeding. He could move the arm, so he knew the bullet had gone straight through without breaking any bones. He could either take the stairs and go at the ones in the basement or handle this one upstairs first. He knew his time was limited, that someone might have heard the gunshots and called the police, but his reputation was at stake. He had never missed a target, so he would never leave until he knew all had been eliminated. He decided to handle the problem upstairs first, him being armed. So, he started towards the closet, ready to end this. He hadn't taken three steps when the closet door burst open. In a blink, he saw the man come out with a gun raised and let off two shots aimed at the man's heart.

Chris felt two shots hit him somewhere in the chest, then he fired his.45 caliber at the shadow coming at him. Jinx froze when she saw a shadow pass by the top of the stairs. Then she heard a loud crash followed by more big gunshots. That was Chris' .45, she thought with hope. Gripping the butt of the Desert Eagles, she took two more steps up. Chris' .45 caliber hollow point caught No Face in the middle of his chest knocking him around. Another two rounds hit him in the lower back sending him stumbling towards the basement door. Jinx was almost at the top step when she saw the figure of a man rush at her from the hallway. By reflex she put both arms up to keep from getting knocked back down the stairs. No Face and Jinx came face to face. She took in his Columbian features and deadly eyes. He took in her bloodied face and bruised head. His eyes widened when their eyes met, and she smiled as he looked down at the two Desert Eagles in his chest. Jinx was holding No Face up with the two guns. She then blew him a kiss and moved both guns under his chin and pulled both triggers at the same time. The blast lifted No Face off his feet and slid him back across the hall floor. Chris saw the hit man stumble toward the basement stairwell, then hesitate at the top. He aimed at the man again, only to see flames spit and then the Desert Eagles roared, and the man's head evaporated. Then he knew it was all over. Chris walked over toward the basement, but passing the upstairs stairwell, a hand grabbed his ankle. He jumped and looked down to see Chan struggling to talk. He dropped to his knees beside the man.

"Is...is...my daughter still alive?" Chan whispered, looking up at Chris.

"Yes, she is safe," Chris answered not really knowing.

"Ok. Good! Now, get me a doctor!" Chan said as he passed out. Chris ran for his cell phone and dialed 9-1-1. Lin and Chris sat in the emergency room holding hands. Connie and Dominique sat across from them silent. They were waiting for Chan to come out of surgery. A top plastic surgeon had been called in for Jinx's face. Chan had been in surgery for three hours. Doctors had given him two blood transfusions because of extensive blood loss. A tall African doctor came out of the ER and walked over to Lin and Chris.

"How is he?" Chris asked.

"He's not out of the woods yet, but we have removed both bullets and re-supplied his loss of blood," the doctor answered.

"The rest is up to his body and God but he's definitely a fighter, so I would say his chances are good."

"Thanks, doc, thanks so much," Chris said as he hugged

Lin in his arms. "I told you he would be ok." They went to see Jinx in another wing. She had a broken wrist, a dislocated shoulder and ten stitches across her jaw that a plastic surgeon had beautifully reconstructed.

"Hey baby, how do you feel?" Lin asked as they entered the room.

"Ok," Jinx answered.

"Just sore as hell. How is Mr. Chan?"

"You know he's a fighter," Chris answered. He could see the relief in Jinx's eyes.

"What's up with you two?" she said looking over at Dominique and Connie.

"Why you so quiet? I know you had a more exciting night that I did," she said.

"Not really," Dominique said, "just some boring ass kissing, that's all, but we were more worried about your butt."

"I'm ok but my face…."

"Baby, you just came out of surgery. He did a wonderful job," Chris said. Jinx nodded her head, closed her eyes and let the drugs take her to sleep. Everyone gave her a kiss and left.

Chapter 43
3 Months Later

Lin was upstairs getting dressed. She was to meet her grandfather and uncle for the first time, and she was nervous. Chris and Chan were downstairs playing Chess as New York watched from the side. CDJ had been sent back to Korea but were planning to return soon. Chan had gotten out of the hospital a week ago and Myra was raising so much fuss about him being gone and getting shot in America that he was leaving for Korea in the morning. Lin heard a horn blow and looked out her window to see two handsome men exiting a white 500 SL Benz. One was young and attractive, white, a deep tan, about 6'1" with black, curly hair. The other was older with his grey hair slicked back. They were her mother's father and half-brother. She had often wondered about her mother's side of the family so now it was time to meet them. She went down to greet them at the front door. Poppa and Tony had made the trip from Columbia to apologize to Chan and talk about business between Chris, Chan and New York. Poppa had been relieved to hear that infamous No Face was dead. Now all he wanted was to be a part of his granddaughter's life. They approached the front door as it was opened by Lin. Poppa stopped in his tracks! Same smile, same beautiful eyes as his Lynn. Lin looked into her grandfather's eyes.

"Hi Poppa. Welcome to my home." Tears blurred Poppa's vision and he couldn't speak as he held his granddaughter for the first time. Chris, Chan and New York stood to greet Poppa and Tony. Chris shook Poppa's hand and nodded at Tony sizing him up.

"Chan, while I catch up with my granddaughter, I think you and Tony have some business to discuss." Poppa said.

"No, Tony and Chris have business to discuss," Chan said. "We will have a drink while you and Lin catch up."

"Tony, this is my right-hand, New York. Let's go to my study to talk." Once inside, Chris turned to Tony, but Tony spoke first.

"Before we start, I just want to apologize for my actions. I hope you understand it was all business," Tony said.

"I do understand," Chris answered. "But where I'm from, if I have a problem with a man, it's with him, not his family. Regardless if we hustlers, drug dealers, dons or lords, we keep it in the streets. Chan gave me the keys to his empire but now that I have Lin, I want out of the game. I been in it too long as it is. As of yesterday, my peoples right here. New York handles everything on our end. We can both lock down the east and west coast. I want all my peeps to stay in their positions. New York will find replacements for the ones killed. So, do we have a deal?" Chris asked.

"Of course," Tony answered. "But one thing. Who is this girl that made No Face's face disappear?"

"Oh, she's just a friend of the family," Chris answered. "One more thing," Chris said. "I will need a million cash from you wired to my account as soon as you get back to Columbia. Can you handle that?"

"Of course," Tony said, "but what's that for?" he asked.

"My future Vice-President," Chris said as they joined the others.

"Everything settled?" Chan asked.

167

"Fo sho," Chris said.

"Tony?" Poppa asked.

"Yes," he answered.

"Well, New York," Chan said, "I hope you ready to ride?"

"I was born ready," New York said smiling.

"Now I would like to put all business aside and get to know my niece," Tony said as Chan poured all of them a drink except, of course, Lin.

"A toast," Chan started. "May our family's blood remain untouched," he said as they all smiled and clicked glasses.

Epilogue

A knock sounded at Mary Davis' front door. "Hold on. I'm coming," she said, making her way through the house. She peeped out the door, looking at a man dressed in a nice suit. "Lord, have mercy, bill collectors again!" She opened the door thinking of another excuse.

"Excuse me. Are you Miss Davis?" the young man asked.

"Yes," she answered.

"May I come in a minute?" he asked.

"Yes, of course. Where are my manners?" They stepped inside her living room as she offered the man a seat. He sat down looking around.

"Miss Davis, my name is Chris Brandin. Your daughter used to work for me at the dealership."

"Yes, I remember her speaking of you, but what's this about?" she asked.

"Miss Davis, I...."

"Please call me Janice."

"Ok, Janice, I just recently found out Alexis had a daughter and I wanted to stop by and let you know that our company has set up a college fund and a lil' something for you also."

"Well, that's real nice of you Chris. I'm sure she would be pleased," she said.

"Ok, well, I don't want to hold you up," Chris said, "but here's my card if you need anything. Please don't hesitate to call. Here's some papers explaining your account numbers and her daughter's."

"Thank you again," she said taking the envelope as Chris left. She opened the envelope and whispered, 'Jesus' as she fell back on her sofa. Alexia's daughter had a million-dollar college fund that paid $500,000 when she turned eighteen and $500,000 when she turned 25 years old. Janice had her own account of $500,000.

Chan went back to Korea and worked on new trade routes with New York and Tony using Chris' contacts on the East coast while locking down the entire West coast and East coast.

Connie, Dominique and Jinx moved to California and opened their own private detective and Security Protection Agency. They are bodyguards to some of Hollywood's biggest names.

Lin finds out she is pregnant. After leaving college for two years, giving birth to a beautiful boy, she returned to college and graduated from Georgetown with honors in Criminal Justice. She opens her own practice in Washington, D.C. and is named one of the top ten high-profile lawyers in the country.

After seeing his son born, Chris moves his money into co-ownerships with New York and another businessman. They bring their own professional baseball team to the triad area and built a new stadium off Interstate 40 in Greensboro. Chris had to change the game to win, but he won.

The End

ABOUT THE AUTHOR

Christopher Allen Walker was born in Virginia, grew up on Allison and Hodges Dairy Rd in Caswell and in Reidsville, North Carolina and now resides in South Lake Tahoe, California. His passion for reading and writing was inspired by best-selling authors, Donald Goines, James Patterson, Dean Koontz, and Toni Morrison.

CPSIA information can be obtained
at www.ICGtesting.com
Printed in the USA
FSHW010502220819
61309FS